The Birthplace

The Birthplace

Henry James

Published by Hesperus Press Limited
28 Mortimer Street, London W1W 7RD
www.hesperuspress.com

The Birthplace first published in 1903

The Private Life first published in *The Atlantic Monthly* in 1892

This edition first published by Hesperus Press, 2012

Foreword © Mark Rylance, 2012

Designed and typeset by Fraser Muggeridge studio
Printed in Jordan by Jordan National Press

ISBN: 978-1-84391-207-1

CONTENTS

FOREWORD

'The shrine at which he was to preside figured to him as the most sacred known to the steps of men, the early home of the supreme poet, the Mecca of the English-speaking race,' so muses Morris Gedge. And, once he and his wife, Isabel, are employed as the keepers of that sacred birthplace, 'He', whose birthplace it was, becomes 'their personal friend, their universal light, their final authority and divinity. Where in the world [...] would they have been without Him?'

With sublime delight, Henry James establishes in *The Birthplace* the religious degree of devotion surrounding William Shakespeare and thereby the resonant parallels of humble origin, sacred birthplace, the established church or 'Body', and the predicament of orthodox fact and fiction that exist between the heavenly saviour Jesus Christ and the earthly saviour William Shakespeare. Like a devout scholar himself, James never uses the name 'Shakespeare', only 'Him' or 'He', but we know about whom he is writing.

Never have the father, son and holy ghost of letters been so splintered by heretics as in the holy trinity – perhaps the holiest literary trinity – of William Shakespeare: his works, his audience, his life. In most publications of these heretical sceptics, so despised by Academia, you will discover a list of famous men and women who, at one time in their life, expressed a doubt that the man born and buried in Stratford-upon-Avon as William *Shakspere* wrote the works attributed to William Shakespeare in 1623. Featured in that list you will find Henry James and his brother, the pioneering psychologist, William James.

Others: Mark Twain, Ralph Waldo Emerson, Orson Welles, Leslie Howard, Tyrone Guthrie, Charlie Chaplin, Sir John Gielgud, Sir Derek Jacobi, Sigmund Freud, Clifton Fadiman, John Galsworthy, Mortimer J. Adler, Paul H. Nitze, Lord Palmerston, William Y. Elliot, Harry A Blackman, Lewis F. Powell Jr., Charles Dickens, Walt Whitman, William James and Henry James.*

Contrary to what you may have read about heretics like these, if you are a friend of Shakespeare I think you will be a friend of James, as, certainly in these stories, and throughout Shakespeare, the conversation revolves around the theme of identity; presumed, mistaken, discovered and, like nature herself, full of secrets. The relationship – indeed the trinity – between an author's creation, an author's apparent personality and an author's audience, is the particular topic of conversation for James. As in Shakespeare's comedies, all is made manifest by love; the love and fascination we have for artists who touch us; the sometimes obsessional desire we have to be intimate with remarkable people. 'The more we *know* Him, [...] the more we shall love Him,' prophecies Morris Gedge.

In *The Private Life* (the companion piece in this volume), this trinity is explored with living characters, including James himself, who relates the tale while also inhabiting it. Inhabiting it intimately, for instance, when he asks, 'What do they call *me*?' and the actress, Blanche Adney, replies, 'You're a searcher of hearts – that frivolous thing an observer.' 'I wish you'd let an observer write you a play!' he breaks out. 'People don't care for what you write: you'd break any run of luck.' 'Well, I see plays all around me,' he replies, 'the air is full of them tonight.'

* See www.doubtaboutwill.org, for what they actually say.

I have read that Henry James longed to be a successful playwright and failed in that ambition. Indeed he records, in his prefaces, a voice that insists sharply to itself, at the moment when the pressure of his frivolous observations can no longer be resisted, 'Dramatise it! Dramatise it!' The more I have read and re-read these stories they have seemed like the works of a dramatist. A dramatist, however, who wrote as many stage directions as words to be spoken, for he so adored the intricate complexity of thought possible between people when words fail, or before words are employed. Take for example this surprise meeting, in the upstairs hall of a Swiss chalet, between our author and the wife of the mysterious Lord Mellifont, Lady Mellifont.

> For a moment, as she stood there, we exchanged two or three ideas that were the more singular for being unspoken. We had caught each other hovering and we understood each other; but as I stepped over to her (so that we were separated from the sitting room by the width of the hall), her lips formed the almost soundless entreaty: 'Don't!' I could see in her conscious eyes everything the word expressed – the confession of her own curiosity and the dread of the consequences of mine. 'Don't!' she repeated as I stood before her. From the moment my experiment could strike her as an act of violence I was ready to renounce it; yet I thought I caught from her frightened face a still deeper betrayal – a possibility of disappointment if I should give way. It was as if she had said: 'I'll let you do it if you'll take the responsibility. Yes, with someone else I'd surprise him. But it would never do for him to think it was I.

This is marvellous stuff for an actress and actor to play but perhaps more suited to an intimate, mind-reading close up on the silver screen than the large proscenium theatres of Henry James's day, still resonating as they were with the eloquent dialogue of Oscar Wilde. Indeed, with *The Heiress* adapted from *Washington Square* in 1947, the cinema and modern drama have proved themselves a wonderful medium for James. I wish these two stories were so adapted.

Intimate mental turmoil, an inner dance of holiday manners in *The Private Life*, becomes, in *The Birthplace*, the labour pains and consequences of new thought, monstrous conception, a concept that could destroy the world!

> 'The whole thing becomes a sort of stiff smug convention, like a dressed-up sacred doll in a Spanish church – which you're a monster if you touch.'

The remark of an inquisitive American visitor in the birthplace.

> 'A monster,' Gedge assented, meeting his eyes.
> The young man smiled, but he thought looking at him a little harder. 'A blasphemer.'
> 'A blasphemer.'

Both stories are spun on the enigma of identity, particularly the identity of writers, though Mr James provides such a vista of what is happening inside the mind, as well as outside in the dialogue, that one is aware of a double-life, to a greater or lesser degree, in all the characters. I like this play of hide and seek. It reminds me that the Shakespeare authorship question is closely related to my own question as to the origin of thoughts and actions in my own psyche and, of course, the proper time and place for the appearance of these inner creations. 'Dramatise it!' Who is it within who commands the 'frivolous observer' James? Did the fact that he had a first name for a surname, a double name, inspire him from an early age to this idea of a creative partnership, a collaboration, a coalition governing his creative psyche? What's in a name? I am indulging my fancy, but there is an observer, who remains anonymous, in most artists I know and I read the author Shakespeare to be profoundly sensitive to this in his sonnets and masked characters (Hamlet, Viola, Rosalind).

The private lives of an aristocrat, Lord Melliflont, who disappears, literally disappears, when not in company, and a successful writer, Claire Vawdrey, whose conversation, though plentiful, lacks any hint of the eloquence of his novels, are the fascination of *The Private Life*. Surprised by a thunderstorm, Vawdrey and James seek refuge in an alpine cowshed. To the narrator's increasing frustration, Vawdrey watches the Byronesque lightning and thunder show, the 'grand rage of nature', all the while regaling his expectant companion with stale anecdotes about the 'celebrated Lady Ringrose'. The lightning projects a hard truth for James: 'For personal relations [Claire Vawdrey] thought his second best good enough.' So, apparently, did gentle Will, endowing to his wife, in the famously uncharacteristic will, his 'second best bed'. 'The world was vulgar and stupid,' James concludes, 'and the real man would have been a fool to come out for it when he could gossip and dine by deputy.' Can James have used the term 'second best' without being aware of its most famous use?

He admits, through his narrator's voice, that he wanted Vawdrey to 'make an exception for *me* – for me all alone, and all handsomely and tenderly, in the vaste horde of the dull'. And I must admit this is an aspect of the Shakespeare authorship question for me and I suspect for others. A deep longing for Shakespeare to make an exception for *me*; to allow me nearer to his true self than any other. And James created Vawdrey from direct experience of a personality in his own time whose 'loud, sound, normal, hearty presence' was at irreconcilable odds with the rich genius of his creation. Eventually James succumbs to the 'whimsical theory of two distinct and alternative presences'.

> Our delightful inconceivable celebrity was double, constructed in two distinct and watertight compartments – one of these figures by the gentleman who sat at a table all alone, silent and unseen, and wrote admirably deep and brave and intricate things; while the gentleman who regularly came forth to sit at a quite different table and substantially and promiscuously and multitudinously dine stood for its companion.

Is this a potential answer to the Shakespeare Authorship question? For many, yes it is. But, can an artist be unlike his art, as Mr Shakspere, in the illiterate records we have of him, stubbornly remains? I will use Shakspere, a frequent spelling of his name, with no disrespect, but only to distinguish now for discussion, the actor from the possible author, Shakespeare. Samuel Schoenbaum, no mere Morris Gedge but a pillar of orthodox Shakespearean biography, despaired 'of ever bridging the vertiginous expanse between the sublimity of the subject and the mundane inconsequence of the documentary record'. Few bardographers even attempt a coherent life narrative, unfolding in chronological order, but relate Shakspere's life by theme, without fair sequence or succession.

Can an artist be unlike his art? Are some of us very different from what we seem? Are all of us? Is the world, the universe in fact, different from what it seems? The great explorers, scientists, innovators in any field are bound to tell us so, from direct experience, or they wouldn't be innovators. Shakespeare tells us so again and again and again. Seeming and Being, the drum and bass of all his songs. And Henry James joins him 'here!', as Morris Gedge would say, stamping his heel into the floorboards of Shakspere's birthplace.

'It seemed to them at first, the offer, too good to be true...' What a beautiful opening to *The Birthplace*. Almost as good as 'Who's there?' upon the battlements of Elsinore. Now the question becomes clear, for Hamlet and for Morris Gedge alike, should one man reveal another man's secret? Many artists, from Al Pacino to J.D. Salinger, have guarded their private lives carefully to liberate their art from autobiographical reduction. Is that what Mr Shakspere did? Did he refrain from ever writing a letter and destroy every letter he received? Did he take care to keep no books and make no notes in any books? Leave no evidence of education, no evidence of having been paid for writing, no extant original manuscript, no handwritten inscriptions, receipts, etc. touching on literary matters? Did he convince all who loved his very successful plays to say nothing at all about him the year he died, though his fellow playwright, Francis Beaumont, who dies in the same year, is interred immediately in Westminster Abbey? Did the man from Stratford hide someone else or just himself?*

The mystery continues and the denial of any mystery grows more vehement. I remember well the occasion, a gathering of the Royal Shakespeare Company in The Swan Theatre, circa 1989, arranged by yours truly; a talk on the true identity of the author of Shakespeare. The first such assembly I ever

* See Diana Price: *Shakespeare's Unorthodox Biography* if you are intrigued.

organised. The reaction? Outrage, to my sincere, if naive, surprise. Yes, I know Morris Gedge well.

James doesn't explore the question which usually follows a discovery such as Gedge's: the discovery of 'the man shaped hole, Shakespeare' (a phrase coined by bardographer Michael Wood): if the facts don't tally in Stratford-upon-Avon, then, who wrote the works? James doesn't peep into that prism. He focuses on the internal effect which occurs when a man, Morris Gedge, perceives a truth beneath the surface appearance, 'the Maya illusion', to quote another sceptic, Walt Whitman. The surface appearance, in this case, being no less than the identity of the inventor of human identity, humanity, to quote Harold Bloom, orthodox bardographer.

The reader, innocent of just what a man-shaped hole exists in the place of the author, may take Gedge for a man on the edge of a nervous breakdown, on the verge of joining the flat earth society (where I and other authorship sceptics belong according to Professor Bloom). He actually joins, if he only knew it, good company.

'I no longer believe that William Shakespeare the actor from Stratford was the author of the works that have been ascribed to him.' – Sigmund Freud

'Other admirable men have led lives in some sort of keeping with their thought, but this man was in wide contrast.' – Ralph Waldo Emerson

'It is a great comfort... that so little is known concerning the poet. The life of William Shakespeare is a fine mystery and I tremble every day lest something should turn up.' – Charles Dickens

'Shall I set down the rest of the conjectures which constitute the giant biography of William Shakespeare? It would strain the Unabridged Dictionary to hold them. He is a Brontosaur: nine bones and six hundred barrels of plaster of paris.' – Mark Twain

and

Henry James himself: 'I am… haunted by the conviction that the divine William is the biggest and most successful fraud ever practised on a patient world.'

Good company or not, the fears of Isabel and Morris Gedge are not unfounded. The modern day 'Body', as James calls them, The Shakespeare Birthplace Trust, has recently launched an authorship campaign: 'Shakespeare Bites Back'. The Revd. Dr Paul Edmondson, head of learning and research, writes:

For true Shakespeareans, there is no question that Shakespeare wrote Shakespeare; no debate; no issue… Some people take the ultimately untenable view that it does not matter who wrote the plays. It matters exceedingly. To say that it does not is to deny history, to allow intellectual theft (for that is one of the often unspoken moral points within the Authorship discussion), to scorn scholarship, to encourage snobbery (the alternative candidates are mainly aristocrats or university educated) and to support misguided biographical readings of the work.

'True Shakespeareans' can now go to a new digital platform and hear 'anti-Stratfordians' mocked and shamed, even psycho-analysed! One such, the first and only professor in England teaching an MA course which considers the Authorship question, has received so much hate mail, he has asked friends to send him a friendly note, just to make a change.

The surprising lack of evidence of a literary life, unlike all other theatre writers of Mr Shakspere's time, as Morris Gedge discovers, makes it difficult for authorities such as Dr Edmondson to be reasonable in the face of doubt. In fact, it is the authorities who have asserted for decades that it does not matter who wrote the plays, while publishing innumerable biographies that level or leap over all the difficult historical details of their candidate's life. They have shunned the principles of scholarship by attempting to repress a reasonable doubt with personal attack and misrepresentation and, as for 'intellectual theft', are we to expect litigation next? Snobbery, they say. When an author writes with expert authority about a large number of matters indigenous to an aristocratic life and with the level of education and travel only available at that time to an aristocrat (or a remarkable common man such as Christopher Marlowe, whom we know attended university), is it snobbery to consider university educated aristocrats as collaborators or authorship candidates? No, it is natural.

I like James' focus though: the mind of Morris Gedge as a birthplace itself undergoing a paradigm shift. Often, perhaps always, the authorship question itself seems inconsequential in the face of humanity's pressing questions. What does it matter? The plays and sonnets exist, delight and escape biographical definition. Rather, their myriad characters and events create a beautiful rainbow of biographical imagination and research. 'The Show' that Morris Gedge is hired to sustain creates a mystery. A fine mystery, thought Charles Dickens. Albert Einstein thought the mysterious the most beautiful aspect of nature the human mind could experience. 'It is the source of all true art and science.' Here now, as we all face the mystery of so many important shifting paradigms in economics, religion, environment, health, etc., 'who wrote Shakespeare' isn't all that important, but the minds and behaviour of those engaging with, and resisting, the possibility that Shakspere didn't write Shakespeare, do become instructive on the wider plane of paradigm change.

'"The play's the thing." Let the author alone.'

'That's just what They won't do', replies Gedge, 'nor let *me* do. It's all I want – to let the author alone. Practically, there *is* no author; that is for us to deal with. There are all the immortal people – *in* the work; but there's nobody else.'

'Yes. That's what it comes to. There should really, to clear the matter up, be no such person.'

'There *is* no such person.'

'But *wasn't* there – ?'

'There was somebody. But They've killed Him. And, dead as He is, They keep it up. They do it over again. They kill him every day.'

'Then if there's no author, if there's nothing to be said but that there isn't anybody, why in the world should there be a house?'

'There shouldn't,' said Morris Gedge.

And in this little dialogue, which I have reduced to its essence, you have a prophecy of the major contortions of the larger, worldwide 'Body', The Orthodox Shakespeare Academy, during the last fifty years; the death of the author; the liberation of innumerable fictions, novels dressed smartly as biography; and now, in James Shapiro's popular book, *Contested Will*, the proposition, more or less, that the birthplace, and all its associated 'fanthistory' of the author, be pulled down.

It seems to me that the natural movement of any such 'Body' would be to embrace the possibility that even if someone else was involved, some other author or authors, they pointed us to Stratford-upon-Avon as a doorway, an entry, for those who are curious about the authorship. Whoever wrote the works, William Shakspere too, they hid themselves and put forth an image of the creator, William Shake-speare, of Stratford upon Avon. Stratford will always be the doorway into the mystery. The portal. This question need not be anti-Stratfordian. So let's start here and move deeper if we enjoy it.

What a wise and generous move it would be for the 'Body', The Shakespeare Birthplace Trust, if they admitted that the authorship has always been a 'fine mystery'; from the enormous vocabulary employed in the writing to the early rumours of concealed authorship amongst Shakespeare's contemporaries: Robert Greene, Thomas Nashe, John Marston, Ben Jonson, Gabriel Harvey. What a pleasure it would be to visit Stratford and see a confident exhibition on the Authorship question! Think of all the Elizabethan characters one would learn about and all the eccentric researchers who have, at one time or another, put forward an overly enthusiastic theory. Who knows it might even boost the tourist industry! I can see tour buses setting off from the back of the birthplace to The Earl Oxford's Hedingham Castle or Francis Bacon's Gorhambury House or even The Countess of Pembroke's Wilton House on the banks of the other River Avon in Wiltshire. What an industry it could be! What a killing they could make!

'The receipts. It appears, speak – ?' [Gedge] was nursing his effect; Isabel intently watched him and the others hung on his lips. 'Yes, speak – ?'

'Well, volumes. They tell the truth.'

At this Mr Hayes laughed again. 'Oh *they* at least do?'

I don't have direct evidence of Henry James taking a tour to Stratford, but I assume he did. His brother, William, writes of a visit in a letter to Charles Eliot Norton, 2nd May 1902.

We [William, and perhaps Henry] went to Stratford for the first time. The absolute extermination and obliteration of every record of Shakespeare save a few sordid material details, and the general suggestion of narrowness and niggardliness which ancient Stratford makes, taken in comparison with the way in which the spiritual quantity 'Shakespeare' has mingled into the soul of the world, was most uncanny, and I feel ready to believe in almost any mythical story of the authorship. In fact a visit to Stratford now seems to me the strongest appeal a Baconian can make.

Nature abhors a vacuum and Henry James relishes the effect on Gedge after he has been purged of his heretic behaviour by his employer, Mr Grant-Jackson, he of the broad well-fitted back, the back of a banker and a patriot. Morris Gedge, like so many bardographers since, becomes truly 'great' when he fills the void with his fantasy. Gedge's show, his hearthside chat, within the hallowed walls of the birthplace, is a creative masterpiece; giving away nothing, summoning up an intimate presence of little Will Shakespeare and then slipping in the customary plasterer's stepladder of bardolatry, the suggestion that there might have been, could have have been, would have been, was, some such 'rudely bound volume of chronicles', no doubt by Holinshed, 'we may be sure, in His father's window seat'. And instantly a glove maker's abode becomes the cradle of human consciousness in the western world and the window seat looks out on the history of Britain, France, Italy, Ancient Egypt, Ancient Greece and Rome, rather than the pile of dung that was all we know for certain. Genius.

Morris himself has become the genius he could not find at the birthplace. His genius has been acknowledged by his charming American guests, Mr and Mrs Hayes of New York City. 'Of course you're tremendously talked about. You've gone round the world.' 'They rave about you.' Many men and women have become 'great' by stepping into the man-shaped hole. Is this why the question still upsets people so? Are the heretics actually not robbing Shakspere of his greatness, but rather the bardographers of their assumed and inhabited greatness?

The show goes on and on and on and even raises a fresh anxiety that an excess of enthusiasm for the show might appear heretic. 'Don't they want then *any* truth – none even for the mere look of it?' asks Mrs Hayes standing in the hallowed birthplace. 'The look of it,' said Morris Gedge, 'is what I give!' Henry James originally imagined, and recorded in his note-books, an ending for Morris Gedge that is different from the one he eventually employed, but I must desist and let you discover the truth behind the devastating ending. 'The very echoes of the Birthplace were themselves, for the instant, hushed,' James imagines, as he gives the last word to Morris Gedge, 'And there *you* are!' And here we are right now, with James, behind the broad well-fitted back of Mr Grant-Jackson, the back of a banker and a patriot, the back of the 'Body', the back of the Shakespeare Birthplace Trust, reading what they would brand heresy.

Henry James discovers two men 'constructed in two distinct and watertight compartments' in *The Private Life* and makes Stratford-upon-Avon a psychological birthplace for Morris and Isabel Gedge, never actually naming the town or its famous son. Stratford has the same power for me. As a teenager, I fell in love with Shakespeare there. As a young RSC actor I wandered along the river in an imagined intimacy with Will. I rollerskated through the empty shopping streets late at night in the same reverie and gradually woke, while there, to the artifice of it all, the market town, the tourism, the beautiful face of it all and the mystery behind that face.

In the Hopi nation of indigenous tribal people, when a young man discovered that the Katchinas, the gods who danced into town and commended or criticised them during childhood, were actually just adult members of the tribe in beautiful masks and costumes, this discovery was a birth; a rite of passage like Orlando's, or Orsino's, or nearly all the characters in *Cymbeline* or *The Tempest*. There was no shame or tearing down of the Katchinas. No, the unmasking was a vital part of growing up. An awakening to the energy, the spirit, the life, the mysterious, what you will, within the apparent dance of nature. The unmasking was done by the adult wearing the mask in a specific time and place. I wonder if such a time and place awaits us. I hope you will agree with me that Henry James writes two of the most enjoyable encounters with the mask of identity that I have had the pleasure to read.

– Mark Rylance, 2012

The Birthplace

It seemed to them at first, the offer, too good to be true, and their friend's letter, addressed to them to feel, as he said, the ground, to sound them as to inclinations and possibilities, had almost the effect of a brave joke at their expense. Their friend, Mr Grant-Jackson, a highly preponderant, pushing person, great in discussion and arrangement, abrupt in overture, unexpected, if not perverse, in attitude, and almost equally acclaimed and objected to in the wide midland region to which he had taught, as the phrase was, the size of his foot – their friend had launched his bolt quite out of the blue and had thereby so shaken them as to make them fear almost more than hope. The place had fallen vacant by the death of one of the two ladies, mother and daughter, who had discharged its duties for fifteen years; the daughter was staying on alone, to accommodate, but had found, though extremely mature, an opportunity of marriage that involved retirement, and the question of the new incumbents was not a little pressing. The want thus determined was of a united couple of some sort, of the right sort, a pair of educated and competent sisters possibly preferred, but a married pair having its advantage if other qualifications were marked. Applicants, candidates, besiegers of the door of everyone supposed to have a voice in the matter, were already beyond counting, and Mr Grant-Jackson, who was in his way diplomatic and whose voice, though not perhaps of the loudest, possessed notes of insist-ence, had found his preference fixing itself on some person or brace of persons who had been decent and dumb. The Gedges appeared to have struck him as waiting in silence – though absolutely, as happened, no busybody had brought them, far away in the north, a hint either of bliss or of danger;

and the happy spell, for the rest, had obviously been wrought in him by a remembrance which, though now scarcely fresh, had never before borne any such fruit.

Morris Gedge had for a few years, as a young man, carried on a small private school of the order known as preparatory, and had happened then to receive under his roof the small son of the great man, who was not at that time so great. The little boy, during an absence of his parents from England, had been dangerously ill, so dangerously that they had been recalled in haste, though with inevitable delays, from a far country – they had gone to America, with the whole continent and the great sea to cross again – and had got back to find the child saved, but saved, as couldn't help coming to light, by the extreme devotion and perfect judgement of Mrs Gedge. Without children of her own, she had particularly attached herself to this tiniest and tenderest of her husband's pupils, and they had both dreaded as a dire disaster the injury to their little enterprise that would be caused by their losing him. Nervous, anxious, sensitive persons, with a pride – as they were for that matter well aware – above their position, never, at the best, to be anything but dingy, they had nursed him in terror and had brought him through in exhaustion. Exhaustion, as befell, had thus overtaken them early and had for one reason and another managed to assert itself as their permanent portion. The little boy's death would, as they said, have done for them, yet his recovery hadn't saved them; with which it was doubtless also part of a shy but stiff candour in them that they didn't regard themselves as having in a more indirect manner laid up treasure. Treasure was not to be, in any form whatever, of their dreams or of their waking sense; and the years that followed had limped under their weight, had now and then rather grievously stumbled, had even barely escaped laying them in

4

the dust. The school had not prospered, had but dwindled to a close. Gedge's health had failed, and, still more, every sign in him of a capacity to publish himself as practical. He had tried several things, he had tried many, but the final appearance was of their having tried him not less. They mostly, at the time I speak of, were trying his successors, while he found himself, with an effect of dull felicity that had come in this case from the mere postponement of change, in charge of the grey town-library of Blackport-on-Dwindle, all granite, fog and female fiction. This was a situation in which his general intelligence – acknowledged as his strong point – was doubtless conceived, around him, as feeling less of a strain than that mastery of particulars in which he was recognised as weak.

It was at Blackport-on-Dwindle that the silver shaft reached and pierced him; it was as an alternative to dispensing dog's-eared volumes the very titles of which, on the lips of innumerable glib girls, were a challenge to his temper, that the wardenship of so different a temple presented itself. The stipend named differed little from the slim wage at present paid him, but even had it been less the interest and the honour would have struck him as determinant. The shrine at which he was to preside – though he had always lacked occasion to approach it – figured to him as the most sacred known to the steps of men, the early home of the supreme poet, the Mecca of the English-speaking race. The tears came into his eyes sooner still than into his wife's while he looked about with her at their actual narrow prison, so grim with enlightenment, so ugly with industry, so turned away from any dream, so intolerable to any taste. He felt as if a window had opened into a great green woodland, a woodland that had a name, glorious, immortal, that was peopled with vivid figures, each of them renowned, and that gave out a murmur, deep as the sound of

5

the sea, which was the rustle in forest shade of all the poetry, the beauty, the colour of life. It would be prodigious that of this transfigured world *he* should keep the key. No – he couldn't believe it, not even when Isabel, at sight of his face, came and helpfully kissed him. He shook his head with a strange smile. 'We shan't get it. Why should we? It's perfect.'

'If we don't he'll simply have been cruel; which is imposs-ible when he has waited all this time to be kind.' Mrs Gedge did believe – she *would*; since the wide doors of the world of poetry had suddenly pushed back for them it was in the form of poetic justice that they were first to know it. She had her faith in their patron; it was sudden, but it was now complete. 'He remembers – that's all; and that's our strength.'

'And what's *his*?' Gedge asked. 'He may *want* to put us through, but that's a different thing from being able. What are our special advantages?'

'Well, that we're just the thing.' Her knowledge of the needs of the case was, as yet, thanks to scant information, of the vaguest, and she had never, more than her husband, stood on the sacred spot; but she saw herself waving a nicely gloved hand over a collection of remarkable objects and saying to a compact crowd of gaping, awestruck persons: 'And now, please, *this* way.' She even heard herself meeting with prompt-ness and decision an occasional inquiry from a visitor in whom audacity had prevailed over awe. She had been once, with a cousin, years before, to a great northern castle, and that was the way the housekeeper had taken them round. And it was not moreover, either, that she thought of herself as a housekeeper: she was well above that, and the wave of her hand wouldn't fail to be such as to show it. This, and much else, she summed up as she answered her mate. 'Our special advantages are that you're a gentleman.'

'Oh!' said Gedge, as if he had never thought of it, and yet as if too it were scarce worth thinking of.

'I see it all,' she went on; 'they've *had* the vulgar – they find they don't do. We're poor and we're modest, but anyone can see what we are.'

Gedge wondered. 'Do you mean –?' More modest than she, he didn't know quite what she meant.

'We're refined. We know how to speak.'

'Do we?' – he still, suddenly, wondered.

But she was, from the first, surer of everything than he; so that when a few weeks more had elapsed and the shade of uncertainty – though it was only a shade – had grown almost to sicken him, her triumph was to come with the news that they were fairly named. 'We're on poor pay, though we manage' – she had on the present occasion insisted on her point. 'But we're highly cultivated, and for them to get *that*, don't you *see*? without getting too much with it in the way of pretensions and demands, must be precisely their dream. We've no social position, but we don't *mind* that we haven't, do we? a bit; which is because we know the difference between realities and shams. We hold to reality, and that gives us common sense, which the vulgar have less than anything, and which yet must be wanted there, after all, as well as anywhere else.'

Her companion followed her, but musingly, as if his horizon had within a few moments grown so great that he was almost lost in it and required a new orientation. The shining spaces surrounded him; the association alone gave a nobler arch to the sky. 'Allow that we hold also a little to the romance. It seems to me that that's the beauty. We've missed it all our life, and now it's come. We shall be at headquarters for it. We shall have our fill of it.'

7

She looked at his face, at the effect in it of these prospects, and her own lighted as if he had suddenly grown handsome. 'Certainly – we shall live as in a fairy-tale. But what I mean is that we shall give, in a way – and so gladly – quite as much as we get. With all the rest of it we're, for instance, neat.' Their letter had come to them at breakfast, and she picked a fly out of the butter-dish. 'It's the way we'll *keep* the place' – with which she removed from the sofa to the top of the cottage-piano a tin of biscuits that had refused to squeeze into the cupboard. At Blackport they were in lodgings – of the lowest description, she had been known, with a freedom felt by Blackport to be slightly invidious, to declare. The Birthplace – and that itself, after such a life, was exaltation – wouldn't be lodgings, since a house close beside it was set apart for the warden, a house joining onto it as a sweet old parsonage is often annexed to a quaint old church. It would all together be their home, and such a home as would make a little world that they would never want to leave. She dwelt on the gain, for that matter, to their income; as, obviously, though the salary was not a change for the better, the house, given them, would make all the difference. He assented to this, but absently, and she was almost impatient at the range of his thoughts. It was as if something, for him – the very swarm of them – veiled the view; and he presently, of himself, showed what it was.

'What I can't get over is its being such a man –!' He almost, from inward emotion, broke down.

'Such a man –?'

'Him, *him*, HIM –!' It was too much.

'Grant-Jackson? Yes, it's a surprise, but one sees how he has been meaning, all the while, the right thing by us.'

'I mean *Him*,' Gedge returned more coldly; 'our becoming familiar and intimate – for that's what it will come to. We shall just live with Him.'

'Of course – it is the beauty.' And she added quite gaily: 'The more we do the more we shall love Him.'

'No doubt – but it's rather awful. The more we *know* Him,' Gedge reflected, 'the more we shall love Him. We don't as yet, you see, know Him so very tremendously.'

'We do so quite as well, I imagine, as the sort of people they've had. And that probably isn't – unless you care, as we do – so awfully necessary. For there are the facts.'

Yes – there are the facts.'

'I mean the principal ones. They're all that the people – the people who come – want.'

'Yes – they must be all *they* want.'

'So that they're all that those who've been in charge have needed to know.'

'Ah,' he said as if it were a question of honour, '*we* must know everything.'

She cheerfully acceded: she had the merit, he felt, of keeping the case within bounds. 'Everything. But about him personally,' she added, 'there isn't, is there? so very, very much.'

'More, I believe, than there used to be. They've made discoveries.'

It was a grand thought. 'Perhaps *we* shall make some!'

'Oh, I shall be content to be a little better up in what has been done.' And his eyes rested on a shelf of books, half of which, little worn but much faded, were of the florid 'gift' order and belonged to the house. Of those among them that were his own most were common specimens of the reference sort, not excluding an old Bradshaw and a catalogue of the town-library. 'We've not even a Set of our own. Of the Works,' he explained in quick repudiation of the sense, perhaps more obvious, in which she might have taken it.

9

As a proof of their scant range of possessions this sounded almost abject, till the painful flush with which they met on the admission melted presently into a different glow. It was just for that kind of poorness that their new situation was, by its intrinsic charm, to console them. And Mrs Gedge had a happy thought. 'Wouldn't the Library more or less have them?'

'Oh no, we've nothing of that sort: for what do you take us?' This, however, was but the play of Gedge's high spirits: the form both depression and exhilaration most frequently took with him being a bitterness on the subject of the literary taste of Blackport. No one was so deeply acquainted with it. It acted with him in fact as so lurid a sign of the future that the charm of the thought of removal was sharply enhanced by the prospect of escape from it. The institution he served didn't of course deserve the particular reproach into which his irony had flowered; and indeed if the several Sets in which the Works were present were a trifle dusty, the dust was a little his own fault. To make up for that now he had the vision of immediately giving his time to the study of them; he saw himself indeed, inflamed with a new passion, earnestly commenting and collating. Mrs Gedge, who had suggested that they ought, till their move should come, to read Him regularly of an evening – certain as they were to do it still more when in closer quarters with Him – Mrs Gedge felt also, in her degree, the spell; so that the very happiest time of their anxious life was perhaps to have been the series of lamplight hours, after supper, in which, alternately taking the book, they declaimed, they almost performed, their beneficent author. He became speedily more than their author – their personal friend, their universal light, their final authority and divinity. Where in the world, they were already asking themselves, would they have been without him? By the time their appointment arrived in form their relation to

Him had immensely developed. It was amusing to Morris Gedge that he had so lately blushed for his ignorance, and he made this remark to his wife during the last hour they were able to give to their study, before proceeding, across half the country, to the scene of their romantic future. It was as if, in deep, close throbs, in cool after-waves that broke of a sudden and bathed his mind, all possession and comprehension and sympathy, all the truth and the life and the story, had come to him, and come, as the newspapers said, to stay. 'It's absurd,' he didn't hesitate to say, 'to talk of our not "knowing". So far as we don't it's because we're donkeys. He's *in* the thing, over His ears, and the more we get into it the more we're with Him. I seem to myself at any rate,' he declared, 'to *see* Him in it as if He were painted on the wall.'

'Oh, *doesn't* one rather, the dear thing? And don't you feel where it is?' Mrs Gedge finely asked. 'We see Him because we love Him – that's what we do. How can we not, the old darling – with what He's doing for us? There's no light' – she had a sententious turn – 'like true affection.'

'Yes, I suppose that's it. And yet,' her husband mused, 'I see, confound me, the faults.'

'That's because you're so critical. You see them, but you don't mind them. You see them, but you forgive them. You mustn't mention them *there*. We shan't, you know, be there for *that*.'

'Dear no!' he laughed: 'we'll chuck out anyone who hints at them.'

2

If the sweetness of the preliminary months had been great, great too, though almost excessive as agitation, was the wonder of fairly being housed with Him, of treading day and night in the footsteps He had worn, of touching the objects, or at all events the surfaces, the substances, over which His hands had played, which His arms, His shoulders had rubbed, of breathing the air – or something not too unlike it – in which His voice had sounded. They had had a little at first their bewilderments, their disconcertedness; the place was both humbler and grander than they had exactly prefigured, more at once of a cottage and of a museum, a little more archaically bare and yet a little more richly official. But the sense was strong with them that the point of view, for the inevitable ease of the connection, patiently, indulgently awaited them; in addition to which, from the first evening, after closing-hour, when the last blank pilgrim had gone, the mere spell, the mystic presence – as if they had had it quite to themselves – were all they could have desired. They had received, by Grant-Jackson's care and in addition to a table of instructions and admonitions by the number, and in some particulars by the nature, of which they found themselves slightly depressed, various little guides, handbooks, travellers' tributes, literary memorials and other catch-penny publications, which, however, were to be for the moment swallowed up in the interesting episode of the induction or initiation appointed for them in advance at the hands of several persons whose connection with the establishment was, as superior to their own, still more official, and at those in especial of one of the ladies who had for so many years borne the brunt. About the instructions from above, about the shilling books and the well-known facts and the full-blown legend, the supervision, the subjection, the submission, the view as of a cage in which he should circulate and a groove in which he should slide, Gedge had preserved a certain play of mind; but all power of reaction appeared suddenly to desert him in the presence of his so visibly competent predecessor and as an effect of her good offices. He had not the resource, enjoyed by his wife, of seeing himself, with impatience, attired in black silk of a make characterized by just the right shade of austerity; so that this firm, smooth, expert and consummately respectable middle-aged person had him somehow, on the whole ground, completely at her mercy.

It was evidently something of a rueful moment when, as a lesson – she being for the day or two still in the field – he accepted Miss Putchin's suggestion of 'going round' with her and with the successive squads of visitors she was there to deal with. He appreciated her method – he saw there had to be one; he admired her as succinct and definite; for there were the facts, as his wife had said at Blackport, and they were to be disposed of in the time; yet he felt like a very little boy as he dangled, more than once, with Mrs Gedge, at the tail of the human comet. The idea had been that they should, by this attendance, more fully embrace the possible accidents and incidents, as it were, of the relation to the great public in which they were to find themselves; and the poor man's excited perception of the great public rapidly became such as to resist any diversion meaner than that of the admirable manner of their guide. It wandered from his gaping companions to that of the priestess in black silk, whom he kept asking himself if either he or Isabel could hope by any possibility ever remotely to resemble; then it bounded restlessly back to the numerous persons who revealed to him, as it had never yet been revealed, the happy power of the simple to hang upon the lips of the wise. The great thing seemed to be – and quite surprisingly – that the business was easy and the strain, which as a strain they had feared, moderate; so that he might have been puzzled, had he fairly caught himself in the act, by his recognising as the last effect of the impression an odd absence of the ability to rest in it, an agitation deep within him that vaguely threatened to grow. 'It isn't, you see, so very complicated,' the black silk lady seemed to throw off, with everything else, in her neat, crisp, cheerful way; in spite of which he already, the very first time – that is after several parties had been in and out and up and down – went so far as to wonder if there weren't more in it than she imagined. She was, so to speak, kindness itself – was all encouragement and reassurance; but it was just her slightly coarse redolence of these very things that, on repetition, before they parted, dimmed a little, as he felt, the light of his acknowledging smile. That, again, she took for a symptom of some pleading weakness in him – he could never be as brave as she; so that she wound up with a few pleasant words from the very depth of her experience. 'You'll get into it, never fear – it will *come*; and then you'll feel as if you had never done anything else.' He was afterwards to know that, on the spot, at this moment, he must have begun to wince a little at such a menace; that he might come to feel as if he had never done anything but what Miss Putchin did loomed for him, in germ, as a penalty to pay. The support she offered, nonetheless, continued to strike him; she put the whole thing on so sound a basis when she said: 'You see they're so nice about it – they take such an interest. And they never do a thing they shouldn't. That was always everything to mother and me.' 'They', Gedge had already noticed, referred constantly and hugely, in the good woman's talk, to the millions who shuffled through the house;

15

the pronoun in question was forever on her lips, the hordes it represented filled her consciousness, the addition of their numbers ministered to her glory. Mrs Gedge promptly met her. 'It must be indeed delightful to see the effect on so many, and to feel that one may perhaps do something to make it – well, permanent.' But he was kept silent by his becoming more sharply aware that this was a new view, for him, of the reference made, that he had never thought of the quality of the place as derived from Them, but from Somebody Else, and that They, in short, seemed to have got into the way of crowding Him out. He found himself even a little resenting this for Him, which perhaps had something to do with the slightly invidious cast of his next inquiry.

'And are They always, as one might say – a – stupid?'

'Stupid!' She stared, looking as if no one *could* be such a thing in such a connection. No one had ever been anything but neat and cheerful and fluent, except to be attentive and unobjectionable and, so far as was possible, American.

'What I mean is,' he explained, 'is there any perceptible proportion that take an interest in Him?'

His wife stepped on his toe; she deprecated levity. But his mistake fortunately was lost on their friend. 'That's just why they come, that they take such an interest. I sometimes think they take more than about anything else in the world.' With which Miss Putchin looked about at the place. 'It *is* pretty, don't you think, the way they've got it now?' This, Gedge saw, was a different 'They'; it applied to the powers that were – the people who had appointed him, the governing, visiting Body, in respect to which he was afterwards to remark to Mrs Gedge that a fellow – it was the difficulty – didn't know 'where to have her'. His wife, at a loss, questioned at that moment the necessity of having her anywhere, and he said, good-humouredly, 'Of course; it's all right.' He was in fact content enough with the last touches their friend had given the picture. 'There are many who know all about it when they come, and the Americans often are tremendously up. Mother and me really enjoyed' – it was her only slip – 'the interest of the Americans. We've sometimes had ninety a day, and all wanting to see and hear everything. But you'll work them off; you'll see the way – it's all experience.' She came back, for his comfort, to that. She came back also to other things: she did justice to the considerable class who arrived positive and primed. 'There are those who know more about it than you do. But *that* only comes from their interest.'

'Who know more about what?' Gedge inquired.

'Why, about the place. I mean they have their ideas – of what everything is, and *where* it is, and what it isn't, and where it *should* be. They do ask questions,' she said, yet not so much in warning as in the complacency of being seasoned and sound; 'and they're down on you when they think you go wrong. As if you ever could! You know too much,' she sagaciously smiled; 'or you *will*.'

'Oh, you mustn't know *too* much, must you?' And Gedge now smiled as well. He knew, he thought, what he meant.

'Well, you must know as much as anybody else. I claim, at any rate, that I do,' Miss Putchin declared. 'They never really caught me.'

'I'm very sure of *that*,' Mrs Gedge said with an elation almost personal.

'Certainly,' he added, 'I don't want to be caught.' She rejoined that, in such a case, he would have *Them* down on him, and he saw that this time she meant the powers above. It quickened his sense of all the elements that were to reckon with, yet he felt at the same time that the powers above were

17

not what he should most fear. 'I'm glad,' he observed, 'that they ever ask questions; but I happened to notice, you know, that no one did today.'

'Then you missed several – and no loss. There were three or four put to me too silly to remember. But of course they mostly *are* silly.'

'You mean the questions?'

She laughed with all her cheer. 'Yes, sir; I don't mean the answers.'

Whereupon, for a moment snubbed and silent, he felt like one of the crowd. Then it made him slightly vicious. 'I didn't know but you meant the people in general – till I remembered that I'm to understand from you that *they're wise*, only occasionally breaking down.'

It was not really till then, he thought, that she lost patience; and he had had, much more than he meant no doubt, a cross-questioning air. 'You'll see for yourself.' Of which he was sure enough. He was in fact so ready to take this that she came round to full accommodation, put it frankly that every now and then they broke out – not the silly, oh no, the intensely enquiring. 'We've had quite lively discussions, don't you know, about well-known points. They want it all *their* way, and I know the sort that are going to as soon as I see them. That's one of the things you do – you get to know the sorts. And if it's what you're afraid of – their taking you up,' she was further gracious enough to say, 'you needn't mind a bit. What *do* they know, after all, when for us it's our life? I've never moved an inch, because, you see, I shouldn't have been here if I didn't know where I was. No more will *you* be a year hence – you know what I mean, putting it impossibly – if *you* don't. I expect you do, in spite of your fancies.' And she dropped once more to bedrock. 'There are the facts. Otherwise where would any of us be? That's all you've got to go upon. A person, however cheeky, can't have them *his* way just because he takes it into his head. There can only be *one* way, and,' she gaily added as she took leave of them, 'I'm sure it's quite enough!'

3

Gedge not only assented eagerly – one way *was* quite enough if it were the right one – but repeated it, after this conversation, at odd moments, several times over to his wife. 'There can only be one way, one way,' he continued to remark – though indeed much as if it were a joke; till she asked him how many more he supposed she wanted. He failed to answer this question, but resorted to another repetition, 'There are the facts, the facts,' which, perhaps, however, he kept a little more to himself, sounding it at intervals in different parts of the house. Mrs Gedge was full of comment on their clever introductress, though not restrictively save in the matter of her speech, 'Me and mother,' and a general tone – which certainly was not their sort of thing. 'I don't know,' he said, 'perhaps it comes with the place, since speaking in immortal verse doesn't seem to come. It must be, one seems to see, one thing or the other. I dare say that in a few months I shall also be at it – "me and the wife".'

'Why not me and the missus at once?' Mrs Gedge resentfully inquired. 'I don't think,' she observed at another time, 'that I quite know what's the matter with you.'

'It's only that I'm excited, awfully excited – as I don't see how one can not be. You wouldn't have a fellow drop into this berth as into an appointment at the Post Office. Here on the spot it goes to my head; how can that be helped? But we shall live into it, and perhaps,' he said with an implication of the other possibility that was doubtless but part of his fine ecstasy, 'we shall live through it.' The place acted on his imagination – how, surely, shouldn't it? And his imagination acted on his nerves, and these things together, with the general vividness and the new and complete immersion, made rest for him almost impossible, so that he could scarce go to bed at night and even during the first week more than once rose in the small hours to move about, up and down, with his lamp, standing, sitting, listening, wondering, in the stillness, as if positively to recover some echo, to surprise some secret, of the *genius loci*[1]. He couldn't have explained it – and didn't in fact need to explain it, at least to himself, since the impulse simply held him and shook him; but the time after closing, the time above all after the people – Them, as he felt himself on the way to think of them, predominant, insistent, all in the foreground – brought him, or ought to have brought him, he seemed to see, nearer to the enshrined Presence, enlarged the opportunity for communion and intensified the sense of it. These nightly prowls, as he called them, were disquieting to his wife, who had no disposition to share in them, speaking with decision of the whole place as just the place to be forbidding after dark. She rejoiced in the distinctness, contiguous though it was, of their own little residence, where she trimmed the lamp and stirred the fire and heard the kettle sing, repairing the while the omissions of the small domestic who slept out; she foresaw herself with some promptness, drawing rather sharply the line between her own precinct and that in which the great spirit might walk. It would be with them, the great spirit, all day – even if indeed on her making that remark, and in just that form, to her husband, he replied with a queer 'But will he though?' And she vaguely imaged the development of a domestic antidote after a while, precisely, in the shape of curtains more markedly drawn and everything most modern and lively, tea, 'patterns', the newspapers, the female fiction itself that they had reacted against at Blackport, quite defiantly cultivated.

These possibilities, however, were all right, as her companion said it was, all the first autumn – they had arrived at summer's end; as if he were more than content with a special set of his own that he had access to from behind, passing out of their low door for the few steps between it and the Birthplace. With his lamp ever so carefully guarded, and his nursed keys that made him free of treasures, he crossed the dusky interval so often that she began to qualify it as a habit that 'grew'. She spoke of it almost as if he had taken to drink, and he humoured that view of it by confessing that the cup was strong. This had been in truth, altogether, his immediate sense of it; strange and deep for him the spell of silent sessions before familiarity and, to some small extent, disappointment had set in. The exhibitional side of the establishment had struck him, even on arrival, as qualifying too much its character; he scarce knew what he might best have looked for, but the three or four rooms bristled overmuch, in the garish light of day, with busts and relics, not even ostensibly always *His*, old prints and old editions, old objects fashioned in His likeness, furniture 'of the time' and autographs of celebrated worshippers. In the quiet hours and the deep dusk, nonetheless, under the play of the shifted lamp and that of his own emotion, these things too recovered their advantage, ministered to the mystery, or at all events to the impression, seemed consciously to offer themselves as personal to the poet. Not one of them was really or unchallengeably so, but they had somehow, through long association, got, as Gedge always phrased it, into the secret, and it was about the secret he asked them while he restlessly wandered. It was not till months had elapsed that he found how little they had to tell him, and he was quite at his ease with them when he knew they were by no means where his sensibility had first placed them. They were as out of it as he; only, to do them justice, they had made him immensely feel. And still, too, it was not

23

they who had done that most, since his sentiment had gradually cleared itself to deep, to deeper refinements.

The Holy of Holies of the Birthplace was the low, the sublime Chamber of Birth, sublime because, as the Americans usually said – unlike the natives they mostly found words – it was so pathetic; and pathetic because it was – well, really nothing else in the world that one could name, number or measure. It was as empty as a shell of which the kernel has withered, and contained neither busts nor prints nor early copies; it contained only the Fact – *the* Fact itself – which, as he stood sentient there at midnight, our friend, holding his breath, allowed to sink into him. He *had* to take it as the place where the spirit would most walk and where he would therefore be most to be met, with possibilities of recognition and reciprocity. He hadn't, most probably – *He* hadn't – much inhabited the room, as men weren't apt, as a rule, to convert to their later use and involve in their wider fortune the scene itself of their nativity. But as there were moments when, in the conflict of theories, the sole certainty surviving for the critic threatened to be that He had not – unlike other successful men – *not* been born, so Gedge, though little of a critic, clung to the square feet of space that connected themselves, however feebly, with the positive appearance. He was little of a critic – he was nothing of one; he hadn't pretended to the character before coming, nor come to pretend to it; also, luckily for him, he was seeing day by day how little use he could possibly have for it. It would be to him, the attitude of a high expert, distinctly a stumbling-block, and that he rejoiced, as the winter waned, in his ignorance, was one of the propositions he betook himself, in his odd manner, to enunciating to his wife. She denied it, for hadn't she, in the first place, been present, wasn't she still present, at his pious, his tireless study of everything connected with the subject? – so present that she had herself learned more about it than had ever seemed likely. Then, in the second place, he was not to proclaim on the housetops any point at which he might be weak, for who knew, if it should get abroad that they were ignorant, what effect might be produced – ?

'On the attraction' – he took her up – 'of the Show?'

He had fallen into the harmless habit of speaking of the place as the 'Show'; but she didn't mind this so much as to be diverted by it. 'No; on the attitude of the Body. You know they're pleased with us, and I don't see why you should want to spoil it. We got in by a tight squeeze – you know we've had evidence of that, and that it was about as much as our backers could manage. But we're proving a comfort to them, and it's absurd of you to question your suitability to people who were content with the Putchins.'

'I don't, my dear,' he returned, 'question anything; but if I should do so it would be precisely because of the greater advantage constituted for the Putchins by the simplicity of their spirit. They were kept straight by the quality of their ignorance – which was denser even than mine. It was a mistake in us, from the first, to have attempted to correct or to disguise ours. We should have waited simply to become good parrots, to learn our lesson – all on the spot here, so little of it is wanted – and squawk it off.'

'Ah, "squawk", love – what a word to use about Him!'

'It isn't about Him – nothing's about Him. None of Them care tuppence about Him. The only thing They care about is this empty shell – or rather, for it isn't empty, the extraneous, preposterous stuffing of it.'

'Preposterous?' – he made her stare with this as he had not yet done.

At sight of her look, however – the gleam, as it might have been, of a queer suspicion – he bent to her kindly and tapped her cheek. 'Oh, it's all right. We *must* fall back on the Putchins. Do you remember what she said? – "They've made it so pretty now." They *have* made it pretty, and it's a first-rate show. It's a first-rate show and a first-rate billet, and He was a first-rate poet, and you're a first-rate woman – to put up so sweetly, I mean, with my nonsense.'

She appreciated his domestic charm and she justified that part of his tribute which concerned herself. 'I don't care how much of your nonsense you talk to me, so long as you *keep* it all for me and don't treat *Them* to it.'

'The pilgrims? No,' he conceded – 'it isn't fair to Them. They mean well.'

'What complaint have we, after all, to make of Them so long as They don't break off bits – as They used, Miss Putchin told us, so awfully – to conceal about Their Persons? She broke them at least of that.'

'Yes,' Gedge mused again; 'I wish awfully she hadn't!'

'You would like the relics destroyed, removed? That's all that's wanted!'

'There *are* no relics.'

'There won't be any *soon*, unless you take care.' But he was already laughing, and the talk was not dropped without his having patted her once more. An impression or two, however, remained with her from it, as he saw from a question she asked him on the morrow. 'What did you mean yesterday about Miss Putchin's simplicity – its keeping her "straight"? Do you mean mentally?'

Her 'mentally' was rather portentous, but he practically confessed. 'Well, it kept her up. I mean,' he amended, laughing, 'it kept her down.'

It was really as if she had been a little uneasy. 'You consider there's a danger of your being affected? You know what I mean. Of its going to your head. You do know,' she insisted as he said nothing. 'Through your caring for Him so. You'd certainly be right in that case about its having been a mistake for you to plunge so deep.' And then as his listening without reply, though with his look a little sad for her, might have denoted that, allowing for extravagance of statement, he saw there was something in it: 'Give up your prowls. Keep it for daylight. Keep it for *Them*.'

'Ah,' he smiled, 'if one could! My prowls,' he added, 'are what I most enjoy. They're the only time, as I've told you before, that I'm really with *Him*. Then I don't see the place. He isn't the place.'

'I don't care for what you "don't" see,' she replied with vivacity; 'the question is of what you do see.'

Well, if it was, he waited before meeting it. 'Do you know what I sometimes do?' And then as she waited too: 'In the Birthroom there, when I look in late, I often put out my light. That makes it better.'

'Makes what–?'

'Everything.'

'What is it then you see in the dark?'

'Nothing!' said Morris Gedge.

'And what's the pleasure of that?'

'Well, what the American ladies say. It's so fascinating.'

4

The autumn was brisk, as Miss Putchin had told them it would be, but business naturally fell off with the winter months and the short days. There was rarely an hour indeed without a call of some sort, and they were never allowed to forget that they kept the shop in all the world, as they might say, where custom was least fluctuating. The seasons told on it, as they tell upon travel, but no other influence, consideration or convulsion to which the population of the globe is exposed. This population, never exactly in simultaneous hordes, but in a full, swift and steady stream, passed through the smoothly-working mill and went, in its variety of degrees duly impressed and edified, on its artless way. Gedge gave himself up, with much ingenuity of spirit, to trying to keep in relation with it; having even at moments, in the early time, glimpses of the chance that the impressions gathered from so rare an opportunity for contact with the general mind might prove as interesting as anything else in the connection. Types, classes, nationalities, manners, diversities of behaviour, modes of seeing, feeling, of expression, would pass before him and become for him, after a fashion, the experience of an untravelled man. His journeys had been short and saving, but poetic justice again seemed inclined to work for him in placing him just at the point in all Europe perhaps where the confluence of races was thickest. The theory, at any rate, carried him on, operating helpfully for the term of his anxious beginnings and gilding in a manner – it was the way he characterized the case to his wife – the somewhat stodgy gingerbread of their daily routine. They had not known many people, and their visiting-list was small – which made it again poetic justice that they should be visited on such a scale. They dressed and were at home, they were under arms and received, and except for the offer of refreshment – and Gedge had his view that there would eventually be a *buffet* farmed out to a great firm – their hospitality would have made them princely if mere hospitality ever did. Thus they were launched, and it was interesting, and from having been ready to drop, originally, with fatigue, they emerged even-winded and strong in the legs, as if they had had an Alpine holiday. This experience, Gedge opined, also represented, as a gain, a like seasoning of the spirit – by which he meant a certain command of impenetrable patience.

The patience was needed for the particular feature of the ordeal that, by the time the lively season was with them again, had disengaged itself as the sharpest – the immense assumption of veracities and sanctities, of the general sound-ness of the legend with which everyone arrived. He was well provided, certainly, for meeting it, and he gave all he had, yet he had sometimes the sense of a vague resentment on the part of his pilgrims at his not ladling out their fare with a bigger spoon. An irritation had begun to grumble in him during the comparatively idle months of winter when a pilgrim would turn up singly. The pious individual, entertained for the half-hour, had occasionally seemed to offer him the promise of beguilement or the semblance of a personal relation; it came back again to the few pleasant calls he had received in the course of a life almost void of social amenity. Sometimes he liked the person, the face, the speech: an educated man, a gentleman, not one of the herd; a graceful woman, vague, accidental, unconscious of him, but making him wonder, while he hovered, who she was. These chances represented for him light yearnings and faint flutters; they acted indeed, within him, in a special, an extraordinary way. He would have liked to talk with such stray companions, to talk with them *really*, to talk with them as he might have talked if he had met them where he couldn't meet them – at dinner, in the 'world', on a visit at a country-house. Then he could have said – and about the shrine and the idol always – things he couldn't say now. The form in which his irritation first came to him was that of his feeling obliged to say to them – to the single visitor, even when sympathetic, quite as to the gaping group – the particular things, a dreadful dozen or so, that they expected. If he had thus arrived at characterising these things as dreadful the reason touches the very point that, for a while turning everything over, he kept dodging, not facing, trying to ignore. The point was that he was on his way to become two quite different persons, the public and the private, and yet that it would somehow have to be managed that these persons should live together. He was splitting into halves, unmistakably – he who, whatever else he had been, had at least always been so entire and in his way, so solid. One of the halves, or perhaps even, since the split promised to be rather unequal, one of the quarters, was the keeper, the showman, the priest of the idol; the other piece was the poor unsuccessful honest man he had always been.

There were moments when he recognised this primary character as he had never done before; when he in fact quite shook in his shoes at the idea that it perhaps had in reserve some supreme assertion of its identity. It was honest, verily, just by reason of the possibility. It was poor and unsuccessful because here it was just on the verge of quarrelling with its bread and butter. Salvation would be of course – the salvation of the showman – rigidly to *keep* it on the verge; not to let it, in other words, overpass by an inch. He might count on this, he said to himself, if there weren't any public – if there weren't thousands of people demanding of him what he was paid for. He saw the approach of the stage at which they would affect him, the thousands of people – and perhaps even more the earnest individual – as coming really to see if he were earning his wage. Wouldn't he soon begin to fancy them in league with the Body, practically deputed by it – given, no doubt, a kindled suspicion to look in and report observations? It was the way he broke down with the lonely pilgrim that led to his first heart-searchings – broke down as to the courage required for damping an uncritical faith. What they all most wanted was to feel that everything was 'just as it was'; only the shock of having to part with that vision was greater than any individual could bear unsupported. The bad moments were upstairs in the Birthroom, for here the forces pressing on the very edge assumed a dire intensity. The mere expression of eye, all-credulous, omnivorous and fairly moistening in the act, with which many persons gazed about, might eventually make it difficult for him to remain fairly civil. Often they came in pairs – sometimes one had come before – and then they explained to each other. He never in that case corrected; he listened, for the lesson of listening: after which he would remark to his wife that there was no end to what he was learning. He saw that if he should really ever break down it would be with her he would begin. He had given her hints and digs enough, but she was so inflamed with appreciation that she either didn't feel them or pretended not to understand.

This was the greater complication that, with the return of the spring and the increase of the public, her services were more required. She took the field with him, from an early hour; she was present with the party above while he kept an eye, and still more an ear, on the party below; and how could he know, he asked himself, what she might say to them and what she might suffer *Them* to say – or in other words, poor wretches, to believe – while removed from his control? Some day or other, and before too long, he couldn't but think, he must have the matter out with her – the matter, namely, of the morality of their position. The *morality* of women was special – he was getting lights on that. Isabel's conception of her office was to cherish and enrich the legend. It was already, the legend, very taking, but what was she there for but to make it more so? She certainly wasn't there to chill any natural piety. If it was all in the air – all in their 'eye', as the vulgar might say – that He *had* been born in the Birthroom, where was the value of the sixpences they took? Where the equivalent they had engaged to supply? 'Oh dear, yes – just about *here*'; and she must tap the place with her foot. 'Altered? Oh dear, no – save in a few trifling particulars; you see the place – and isn't that just the charm of it? – quite as *He* saw it. Very poor and homely, no doubt; but that's just what's so wonderful.' He didn't want to hear her, and yet he didn't want to give her her head; he didn't want to make difficulties or to snatch the bread from her mouth. But he must nonetheless give her a warning before they had gone *too* far. That was the way, one evening in June, he put it to her; the affluence, with the finest weather, having lately been of the largest, and the crowd, all day, fairly gorged with the story. 'We mustn't, you know, go *too* far.'

The odd thing was that she had now ceased to be even conscious of what troubled him – she was so launched in her own career. 'Too far for what?'

'To save our immortal souls. We mustn't, love, tell too many lies.'

She looked at him with dire reproach. 'Ah now, are you going to begin again?'

'I never *have* begun; I haven't wanted to worry you. But, you know, we don't know anything about it.' And then as she stared, flushing: 'About His having been born up there. About anything, really. Not the least little scrap that would weigh, in any other connection, as evidence. So don't rub it in so.'

'Rub it in how?'

'That He *was* born –' But at sight of her face he only sighed. 'Oh dear, oh dear!'

'Don't you think,' she replied cuttingly, 'that He was born anywhere?'

He hesitated – it was such an edifice to shake. 'Well, we don't know. There's very little *to* know. He covered His tracks as no other human being has ever done.'

She was still in her public costume and had not taken off the gloves that she made a point of wearing as a part of that uniform; she remembered how the rustling housekeeper in the Border castle, on whom she had begun by modelling herself, had worn them. She seemed official and slightly distant. 'To cover His tracks, He must have had to exist. Have we got to give *that* up?'

'No, I don't ask you to give it up *yet*. But there's very little to go upon.'

'And is that what I'm to tell Them in return for everything?'

Gedge waited – he walked about. The place was doubly still after the bustle of the day, and the summer evening rested on it as a blessing, making it, in its small state and ancientry, mellow and sweet. It was good to be there, and it would be good to stay. At the same time there was something incalculable in the effect on one's nerves of the great gregarious density. That was an attitude that had nothing to do with degrees and shades, the attitude of wanting all or nothing.

And you couldn't talk things over with it. You could only do this with friends, and then but in cases where you were sure the friends wouldn't betray you. 'Couldn't you adopt,' he replied at last, 'a slightly more discreet method? What we can say is that things have been *said*; that's all *we* have to do with. "And is this really" – when they jam their umbrellas into the floor – "the very *spot* where He was born?" "So it has, from a long time back, been described as being." Couldn't one meet Them to be decent a little, in some such way as that?'

She looked at him very hard. 'Is that the way *you* meet them?'

'No; I've kept on lying – without scruple, without shame.'

'Then why do you haul me up?'

'Because it has seemed to me that we might, like true companions, work it out a little together.'

This was not strong, he felt, as, pausing with his hands in his pockets, he stood before her; and he knew it as weaker still after she had looked at him a minute. 'Morris Gedge, I propose to be *your* true companion, and I've come here to stay. That's all I've got to say.' It was not, however, for 'You had better try yourself and see,' she presently added. 'Give the place, give the story away, by so much as a look, and – well, I'd allow you about nine days. Then you'd see.'

He feigned, to gain time, an innocence. 'They'd take it so ill?' And then, as she said nothing: 'They'd turn and rend me? They'd tear me to pieces?'

But she wouldn't make a joke of it. 'They wouldn't *have* it, simply.'

'No – they wouldn't. That's what I saw. They won't.'

'You had better,' she went on, 'begin with Grant-Jackson. But even that isn't necessary. It would get to him, it would get to the Body, like wildfire.'

'I see,' said poor Gedge. And indeed for the moment he did see, while his companion followed up what she believed her advantage.

'Do you consider it's *all* a fraud?'

'Well, I grant you there was somebody. But the details are naught. The links are missing. The evidence – in particular about that room upstairs, in itself our Casa Santa – is *nil*. It was so awfully long ago.' Which he knew again sounded weak.

'Of course it was awfully long ago – that's just the beauty and the interest. Tell Them, *tell* Them,' she continued, 'that the evidence is *nil*, and I'll tell them something else.' She spoke it with such meaning that his face seemed to show a question, to which she was on the spot of replying 'I'll tell them that you're a –' She stopped, however, changing it. 'I'll tell them exactly the opposite. And I'll find out what you say – it won't take long – to do it. If we tell different stories, *that* possibly may save us.'

'I see what you mean. It would perhaps, as an oddity, have a success of curiosity. It might become a draw. Still, they but want broad masses.' And he looked at her sadly. 'You're no more than one of Them.'

'If it's being no more than one of them to love it,' she answered, 'then I certainly am. And I am not ashamed of my company.'

'To love *what*?' said Morris Gedge.

'To love to think He was born there.'

'You think too much. It's bad for you.' He turned away with his chronic moan. But it was without losing what she called after him.

'I decline to let the place down.' And what was there indeed to say? They *were* there to keep it up.

5

He kept it up through the summer, but with the queerest consciousness, at times, of the want of proportion between his secret rage and the spirit of those from whom the friction came. He said to himself – so sore as his sensibility had grown – that They were gregariously ferocious at the very time he was seeing Them as individually mild. He said to himself that They were mild only because *he* was – he flattered himself that he was divinely so, considering what he might be; and that he should, as his wife had warned him, soon enough have news of it were he to deflect by a hair's breadth from the line traced for him. *That* was the collective fatuity – that it was capable of turning, on the instant, both to a general and to a particular resentment. Since the least breath of discrimination would get him the sack without mercy, it was absurd, he reflected, to speak of his discomfort as light. He was gagged, he was goaded, as in omnivorous companies he doubtless sometimes showed by a strange silent glare. They would get him the sack for that as well if he didn't look out; therefore wasn't it in effect ferocity when you mightn't even hold your tongue? They wouldn't let you off with silence – They insisted on your committing yourself. It was the pound of flesh – They *would* have it; so under his coat he bled. But a wondrous peace, by exception, dropped on him one afternoon at the end of August. The pressure had, as usual, been high, but it had diminished with the fall of day, and the place was empty before the hour for closing. Then it was that, within a few minutes of this hour, there presented themselves a pair of pilgrims to whom in the ordinary course he would have remarked that they were, to his regret, too late. He was to wonder afterwards why the course had, at sight of the visitors – a gentleman and a lady, appealing and fairly young – shown for him as other than ordinary; the consequence sprang doubtless from something rather fine and unnameable, something, for instance, in the tone of the young man, or in the light of his eye, after hearing the statement on the subject of the hour. 'Yes, we know it's late; but it's just, I'm afraid, *because* of that. We've had rather a notion of escaping the crowd – as, I suppose, you mostly have one now; and it was really on the chance of finding you alone –!'

These things the young man said before being quite admitted, and they were words that anyone might have spoken who had not taken the trouble to be punctual or who desired, a little ingratiatingly, to force the door. Gedge even guessed at the sense that might lurk in them, the hint of a special tip if the point were stretched. There were no tips, he had often thanked his stars, at the Birthplace; there was the charged fee and nothing more; everything else was out of order, to the relief of a palm not formed by nature for a scoop. Yet in spite of everything, in spite especially of the almost audible chink of the gentleman's sovereigns, which might in another case exactly have put him out, he presently found himself, in the Birthroom, access to which he had gracefully enough granted, almost treating the visit as personal and private. The reason – well, the reason would have been, if anywhere, in something naturally persuasive on the part of the couple, unless it had been, rather, again, in the way the young man, once he was in place, met the caretaker's expression of face, held it a moment and seemed to wish to sound it. That they were Americans was promptly clear, and Gedge could very nearly have told what kind; he had arrived at the point of distinguishing kinds, though the difficulty might have been with him now that the case before him was rare. He saw it, in fact, suddenly, in the light of the golden midland evening, which reached them through low old windows, saw it with a rush of feeling, unexpected and smothered, that made him wish for a moment to keep it before him as a case of inordinate happiness. It made him feel old, shabby, poor, but he watched it no less intensely for its doing so. They were children of fortune, of the greatest, as it might seem to Morris Gedge, and they were of course lately married; the husband, smooth-faced and soft, but resolute and fine, several years older than the wife, and the wife vaguely, delicately, irregularly, but mercilessly pretty. Somehow, the world was theirs; they gave the person who took the sixpences at the Birthplace such a sense of the high luxury of freedom as he had never had. The thing was that the world was theirs not simply because they had money – he had seen rich people enough – but because they could in a supreme degree think and feel and say what they liked. They had a nature and a culture, a tradition, a facility of some sort – and all producing in them an effect of positive beauty – that gave a light to their liberty and an ease to their tone. These things moreover suffered nothing from the fact that they happened to be in mourning; this was probably worn for some lately deceased opulent father, or some delicate mother who would be sure to have been a part of the source of the beauty, and it affected Gedge, in the gathered twilight and at his odd crisis, as the very uniform of their distinction.

He couldn't quite have said afterwards by what steps the point had been reached, but it had become at the end of five minutes a part of their presence in the Birthroom, a part of the young man's look, a part of the charm of the moment, and a part, above all, of a strange sense within him of 'Now or never!' that Gedge had suddenly, thrillingly, let himself go. He had not been definitely conscious of drifting to it; he had been, for that, too conscious merely of thinking how different, in all their range, were such a united couple from another united couple that he knew. They were everything he and his wife were not; this was more than anything else the lesson at first of their talk. Thousands of couples of whom the same was true certainly had passed before him, but none of whom it was true with just that engaging intensity. This was *because* of their transcendent freedom; that was what, at the end of five minutes, he saw it all come back to. The husband had been there at some earlier time, and he had his impression, which he wished now to make his wife share. But he already, Gedge could see, had not concealed it from her. A pleasant irony, in fine, our friend seemed to taste in the air – he who had not yet felt free to taste his own.

'I think you weren't here four years ago' – that was what the young man had almost begun by remarking. Gedge liked his remembering it, liked his frankly speaking to him; all the more that he had given him, as it were, no opening. He had let them look about below, and then had taken them up, but without words, without the usual showman's song, of which he would have been afraid. The visitors didn't ask for it; the young man had taken the matter out of his hands by himself dropping for the benefit of the young woman a few detached remarks. What Gedge felt, oddly, was that these remarks were not inconsiderate of him; he had heard others, both of the priggish order and the crude, that might have been called so. And as the young man had not been aided to this cognition of him as new, it already began to make for them a certain common ground. The ground became immense when the visitor presently added with a smile: 'There was a good lady, I recollect, who had a great deal to say.'

It was the gentleman's smile that had done it; the irony was there. 'Ah, there has been a great deal said.' And Gedge's look at his interlocutor doubtless showed his sense of being sounded. It was extraordinary of course that a perfect stranger should have guessed the travail of his spirit, should have caught the gleam of his inner commentary. That probably, in spite of him, leaked out of his poor old eyes. 'Much of it, in such places as this,' he heard himself adding, 'is of course said very irresponsibly.' *Such places as this*! – he winced at the words as soon as he had uttered them.

There was no wincing, however, on the part of his pleasant companions. 'Exactly so; the whole thing becomes a sort of stiff, smug convention, like a dressed-up sacred doll in a Spanish church – which you're a monster if you touch.'

'A monster,' said Gedge, meeting his eyes.

The young man smiled, but he thought he looked at him a little harder. 'A blasphemer.'

'A blasphemer.'

It seemed to do his visitor good – he certainly *was* looking at him harder. Detached as he was, he was interested – he was at least amused. 'Then you don't claim, or at any rate you don't insist – ? I mean you personally.'

He had an identity for him, Gedge felt, that he couldn't have had for a Briton, and the impulse was quick in our friend to testify to this perception. 'I don't insist to *you*.'

The young man laughed. 'It really – I assure you if I may – wouldn't do any good. I'm too awfully interested.'

'Do you mean,' his wife lightly enquired, 'in – a – pulling it down? That is in what you've said to me.'

'Has he said to you,' Gedge intervened, though quaking a little, 'that he would like to pull it down?'

She met, in her free sweetness, this directness with such a charm! 'Oh, perhaps not quite the *house* –!'

'Good. You see we live on it – I mean *we* people.'

The husband had laughed, but had now so completely ceased to look about him that there seemed nothing left for him but to talk avowedly with the caretaker. 'I'm interested,' he explained, 'in what, I think, is *the* interesting thing – or at all events the eternally tormenting one. The fact of the abysmally little that, in proportion, we know.'

'In proportion to what?' his companion asked.

'Well, to what there must have been – to what in fact there *is* – to wonder about. That's the interest; it's immense. He escapes us like a thief at night, carrying off – well, carrying off everything. And people pretend to catch Him like a flown canary, over whom you can close your hand and put Him back. He won't *go* back; he won't *come* back. He's not' – the young man laughed – 'such a fool! It makes Him the happiest of all great men.'

He had begun by speaking to his wife, but had ended, with his friendly, his easy, his indescribable competence, for Gedge – poor Gedge who quite held his breath and who felt, in the most unexpected way, that he had somehow never been in such good society. The young wife, who for herself meanwhile had continued to look about, sighed out, smiled out – Gedge couldn't have told which – her little answer to these remarks. 'It's rather a pity, you know, that He *isn't* here. I mean as Goethe's at Weimar. For Goethe *is* at Weimar.'

'Yes, my dear; that's Goethe's bad luck. There he sticks. *This* man isn't anywhere. I defy you to catch Him.'

'Why not say, beautifully,' the young woman laughed, 'that, like the wind, He's everywhere?'

It wasn't of course the tone of discussion, it was the tone of joking, though of better joking, Gedge seemed to feel, and more within his own appreciation, than he had ever listened to; and this was precisely why the young man could go on without the effect of irritation, answering his wife but still with eyes for their companion. 'I'll be hanged if He's *here*!'

It was almost as if he were taken – that is, struck and rather held – by their companion's unruffled state, which they hadn't meant to ruffle, but which suddenly presented its interest, perhaps even projected its light. The gentleman didn't know, Gedge was afterwards to say to himself, how that hypocrite was inwardly all of a tremble, how it seemed to him that his fate was being literally pulled down on his head. He was trembling for the moment certainly too much to speak; abject he might be, but he didn't want his voice to have the absurdity of a quaver. And the young woman – charming creature! – still had another word. It was for the guardian of the spot, and she made it, in her way, delightful. They had remained in the Holy of Holies, and she had been looking for a minute, with a ruefulness just marked enough to be pretty, at the queer old floor. 'Then if you say it *wasn't* in this room He was born – well, what's the use?'

'What's the use of what?' her husband asked. 'The use, you mean, of our coming here? Why, the place is charming in itself. And it's also interesting,' he added to Gedge, 'to know how you get on.'

Gedge looked at him a moment in silence, but he answered the young woman first. If poor Isabel, he was thinking, could only have been like that! – not as to youth, beauty, arrangement of hair or picturesque grace of hat – these things he didn't mind; but as to sympathy, facility, light perceptive, and yet not cheap, detachment! 'I don't say it wasn't – but I don't say it *was*.'

'Ah, but doesn't that,' she returned, 'come very much to the same thing? And don't They want also to see where He had His dinner and where He had His tea?'

'They want everything,' said Morris Gedge. 'They want to see where He hung up His hat and where He kept His boots and where His mother boiled her pot.'

'But if you don't show them –?'

'They show *me*. It's in all their little books.'

'You mean,' the husband asked, 'that you've only to hold your tongue?'

'I try to,' said Gedge.

'Well,' his visitor smiled, 'I see you *can*.'

Gedge hesitated. 'I can't.'

'Oh, well,' said his friend, 'what does it matter?'

'I do speak,' he continued. 'I can't sometimes not.'

'Then how do you get on?'

Gedge looked at him more abjectly, to his own sense, than he had ever looked at anyone – even at Isabel when she frightened him. 'I don't get on. I speak,' he said, 'since I've spoken to *you*.'

'Oh, we shan't hurt you!' the young man reassuringly laughed.

The twilight meanwhile had sensibly thickened; the end of the visit was indicated. They turned together out of the upper room, and came down the narrow stair. The words just exchanged might have been felt as producing an awkwardness which the young woman gracefully felt the impulse to dissipate. 'You must rather wonder why we've come.' And it was the first note, for Gedge, of a further awkwardness – as if he had definitely heard it make the husband's hand, in a full pocket, begin to fumble.

It was even a little awkwardly that the husband still held off. 'Oh, we like it as it is. There's always *something*.' With which they had approached the door of egress.

'What is there, please?' asked Morris Gedge, not yet opening the door, as he would fain have kept the pair on, and conscious only for a moment after he had spoken that his question was just having, for the young man, too dreadfully wrong a sound. This personage wondered, yet feared, had evidently for some minutes been asking himself; so that, with his preoccupation, the caretaker's words had represented to him, inevitably, 'What is there, please, for *me*?' Gedge already knew, with it, moreover, that he wasn't stopping him in time. He had put his question, to show he himself wasn't afraid, and he must have had in consequence, he was subsequently to reflect, a lamentable air of waiting.

The visitor's hand came out. 'I hope I may take the liberty –?' What afterwards happened our friend scarcely knew, for it fell into a slight confusion, the confusion of a queer gleam of gold – a sovereign fairly thrust at him; of a quick, almost violent motion on his own part, which, to make the matter worse, might well have sent the money rolling on the floor; and then of marked blushes all round, and a sensible embarrassment; producing indeed, in turn, rather oddly, and ever so quickly, an increase of communion. It was as if the young man had offered him money to make up to him for having, as it were, led him on, and then, perceiving the mistake, but liking him the better for his refusal, had wanted to obliterate this aggravation of his original wrong. He had done so, presently, while Gedge got the door open, by saying the best thing he could, and by saying it frankly and gaily. 'Luckily it doesn't at all affect the *work*!'

The small town-street, quiet and empty in the summer eventide, stretched to right and left, with a gabled and timbered house or two, and fairly seemed to have cleared itself to congruity with the historic void over which our friends, lingering an instant to converse, looked at each other. The young wife, rather, looked about a moment at all there wasn't to be seen, and then, before Gedge had found a reply to her husband's remark, uttered, evidently in the interest of conciliation, a little question of her own that she tried to make earnest. 'It's our unfortunate ignorance, you mean, that doesn't?'

'Unfortunate or fortunate. I like it so,' said the husband. '"The play's the thing." Let the author alone.'

Gedge, with his key on his forefinger, leaned against the doorpost, took in the stupid little street, and was sorry to see them go – they seemed so to abandon him. 'That's just what They won't do – not let *me* do. It's all I want – to let the author alone. Practically' – he felt himself getting the last of his chance – 'there *is* no author; that is for us to deal with. There are all the immortal people – *in* the work; but there's nobody else.'

'Yes,' said the young man – 'that's what it comes to. There should really, to clear the matter up, be no such Person.'

'As you say,' Gedge returned, 'it's what it comes to. There *is* no such Person.'

The evening air listened, in the warm, thick midland stillness, while the wife's little cry rang out. 'But *wasn't* there –?'

'There was somebody,' said Gedge, against the doorpost. 'But They've killed Him. And, dead as He is, They keep it up, They do it over again, They kill Him every day.'

He was aware of saying this so grimly – more grimly than he wished – that his companions exchanged a glance and even perhaps looked as if they felt him extravagant. That was the way, really, Isabel had warned him all the others would be looking if he should talk to Them as he talked to *her*. He liked, however, for that matter, to hear how he should sound when pronounced incapable through deterioration of the brain. 'Then if there's no author, if there's nothing to be said but that there isn't anybody,' the young woman smilingly asked, 'why in the world should there be a house?'

'There shouldn't,' said Morris Gedge.

Decidedly, yes, he affected the young man. 'Oh, I don't say, mind you, that you should pull it down!'

'Then where would you *go*?' their companion sweetly enquired.

'That's what my wife asks,' Gedge replied.

'Then keep it up, keep it up!' And the husband held out his hand.

'That's what my wife says,' Gedge went on as he shook it.

The young woman, charming creature, emulated the other visitor; she offered their remarkable friend her handshake. 'Then mind your wife.'

The poor man faced her gravely. 'I would if she were such a wife as you!'

6

It had made for him, all the same, an immense difference; it had given him an extraordinary lift, so that a certain sweet aftertaste of his freedom might, a couple of months later, have been suspected of aiding to produce for him another, and really a more considerable, adventure. It was an odd way to think of it, but he had been, to his imagination, for twenty minutes in good society – that being the term that best described for him the company of people to whom he hadn't to talk, as he further phrased it, rot. It was his title to good society that he had, in his doubtless awkward way, affirmed; and the difficulty was just that, having affirmed it, he couldn't take back the affirmation. Few things had happened to him in life, that is few that were agreeable, but at least *this* had, and he wasn't so constructed that he could go on as if it hadn't. It was going on as if it had, however, that landed him, alas! in the situation unmistakeably marked by a visit from Grant-Jackson, late one afternoon towards the end of October. This had been the hour of the call of the young Americans. Every day that hour had come round something of the deep throb of it, the successful secret, woke up; but the two occasions were, of a truth, related only by being so intensely opposed. The secret had been successful in that he had said nothing of it to Isabel, who, occupied in their own quarter while the incident lasted, had neither heard the visitors arrive nor seen them depart. It was on the other hand scarcely successful in guarding itself from indirect betrayals. There were two persons in the world, at least, who felt as he did; they were persons, also, who had treated him, benignly, as feeling as they did, who had been ready in fact to overflow in gifts as a sign of it, and though they were now off in space they were still with him sufficiently in spirit to make him play, as it were, with the sense of their sympathy. This in turn made him, as he was perfectly aware, more than a shade or two reckless, so that, in his reaction from that gluttony of the public for false facts which had from the first tormented him, he fell into the habit of sailing, as he would have said, too near the wind, or in other words – all in presence of the people – of washing his hands of the legend. He had crossed the line – he knew it; he had struck wild – They drove him to it; he had substituted, by a succession of uncontrollable profanities, an attitude that couldn't be understood for an attitude that but too evidently *had* been.

This was of course the franker line, only he hadn't taken it, alas! for frankness – hadn't in the least, really, *taken* it, but had been simply himself caught up and disposed of by it, hurled by his fate against the bedizened walls of the temple, quite in the way of a priest possessed to excess of the god, or, more vulgarly, that of a blind bull in a china-shop – an animal to which he often compared himself. He had let himself fatally go, in fine, just for irritation, for rage, having, in his predicament, nothing at all to do with frankness – a luxury reserved for quite other situations. It had always been his sentiment that one lived to learn; he had learned something every hour of his life, though people mostly never knew what, in spite of its having generally been – hadn't it? – at somebody's expense. What he was at present continually learning was the sense of a form of words heretofore so vain – the famous 'false position' that had so often helped out a phrase. One used names in that way without knowing what they were worth; then of a sudden, one fine day, their meaning was bitter in the mouth. This was a truth with the relish of which his fireside hours were occupied, and he was quite conscious that a man was exposed who looked so perpetually as if something had disagreed with him. The look to be worn at the Birthplace was properly the beatific, and when once it had fairly been missed by those who took it for granted, who, indeed, paid sixpence for it – like the table-wine in provincial France, it was *compris*[2] – one would be sure to have news of the remark.

News accordingly was what Gedge had been expecting – and what he knew, above all, had been expected by his wife, who had a way of sitting at present as with an ear for a certain knock. She didn't watch him, didn't follow him about the house, at the public hours, to spy upon his treachery; and that could touch him even though her averted eyes went through him more than her fixed. Her mistrust was so perfectly expressed by her manner of showing she trusted that he never felt so nervous, never so tried to keep straight, as when she most let him alone. When the crowd thickened and they had of necessity to receive together he tried himself to get off by allowing her as much as possible the word. When people appealed to him he turned to her – and with more of ceremony than their relation warranted: he couldn't help *this* either, if it seemed ironic – as to the person most concerned or most competent. He flattered himself at these moments that no one would have guessed her being his wife; especially as, to do her justice, she met his manner with a wonderful grim bravado – grim, so to say, for himself, grim by its outrageous cheerfulness for the simple-minded. The lore she *did* produce for them, the associations of the sacred spot that she developed, multiplied, embroidered; the things in short she said and the stupendous way she said them! She wasn't a bit ashamed; for why need virtue be ever ashamed? It *was* virtue, for it put bread into his mouth – he meanwhile, on his side, taking it out of hers. He had seen Grant-Jackson, on the October day, in the Birthplace itself – the right setting of course for such an interview; and what occurred was that, precisely, when the scene had ended and he had come back to their own sitting-room, the question she put to him for information was: 'Have you settled it that I'm to starve?'

She had for a long time said nothing to him so straight – which was but a proof of her real anxiety; the straightness of Grant-Jackson's visit, following on the very slight sinuosity of a note shortly before received from him, made tension show for what it was. By this time, really, however, his decision had been taken; the minutes elapsing between his reappearance at the domestic fireside and his having, from the other threshold, seen Grant-Jackson's broad, well-fitted back, the back of a banker and a patriot, move away, had, though few, presented themselves to him as supremely critical. They formed, as it were, the hinge of his door, that door actually ajar so as to show him a possible fate beyond it, but which, with his hand, in a spasm, thus tightening on the knob, he might either open wide or close partly and altogether. He stood, in the autumn dusk, in the little museum that constituted the vestibule of the temple, and there, as with a concentrated push at the crank of a windlass, he brought himself round. The portraits on the walls seemed vaguely to watch for it; it was in their august presence – kept dimly august, for the moment, by Grant-Jackson's impressive check of his application of a match to the vulgar gas – that the great man had uttered, as if it said all, his 'You know, my dear fellow, really –!' He had managed it with the special tact of a fat man, always, when there was *any*, very fine; he had got the most out of the time, the place, the setting, all the little massed admonitions and symbols; confronted there with his victim on the spot that he took occasion to name to him afresh as, to *his* piety and patriotism, the most sacred on earth, he had given it to be understood that in the first place he was lost in amazement and that in the second he expected a single warning now to suffice. Not to insist too much moreover on the question of gratitude, he would let his remonstrance rest, if need be, solely on the question of taste. *As* a matter of taste alone –! But he was surely not to be obliged to follow that up. Poor Gedge indeed would have been sorry to oblige him, for he saw it was precisely to the atrocious taste of unthankfulness that the allusion was made. When he said he wouldn't dwell on what the fortunate occupant of the post owed him for the stout battle originally fought on his behalf, he simply meant he *would*. That was his tact – which, with everything else that had been mentioned, in the scene, to help, really had the ground to itself. The day *had* been when Gedge couldn't have thanked him enough – though he had thanked him, he considered, almost fulsomely – and nothing, nothing that he could coherently or reputably name, had happened since then. From the moment he was pulled up, in short, he had no case, and if he exhibited, instead of one, only hot tears in his eyes, the mystic gloom of the temple either prevented his friend from seeing them or rendered it possible that they stood for remorse. He had dried them, with the pads formed by the base of his bony thumbs, before he went in to Isabel. This was the more fortunate as, in spite of her inquiry, prompt and pointed, he but moved about the room looking at her hard. Then he stood before the fire a little with his hands behind him and his coat-tails divided, quite as the person in permanent possession. It was an indication his wife appeared to take in; but she put nevertheless presently another question. 'You object to telling me what he said?'

'He said "You know, my dear fellow, really –!"'

'And is that all?'

'Practically. Except that I'm a thankless beast.'

'Well!' she responded, not with dissent.

'You mean that I *am*?'

'Are those the words he used?' she asked with a scruple.

Gedge continued to think. 'The words he used were that I give away the Show and that, from several sources, it has come round to Them.'

'As of course a baby would have known!' And then as her husband said nothing: 'Were *those* the words he used?'

'Absolutely. He couldn't have used better ones.'

'Did he call it,' Mrs Gedge enquired, 'the "Show"?'

'Of course he did. The Biggest on Earth.'

She winced, looking at him hard – she wondered, but only for a moment. 'Well, it *is*.'

'Then it's something,' Gedge went on, 'to have given *that* away. But,' he added, 'I've taken it back.'

'You mean you've been convinced?'

'I mean I've been scared.'

'At last, at last!' she gratefully breathed.

'Oh, it was easily done. It was only two words. But here I am.'

Her face was now less hard for him. 'And what two words?'

'"You know, Mr Gedge, that it simply won't do." That was all. But it was the way such a man says them.'

'I'm glad, then,' Mrs Gedge frankly averred, 'that he is such a man. How did you ever think it *could* do?'

'Well, it was my critical sense. I didn't ever know I had one – till They came and (by putting me here) waked it up in me. Then I had, somehow, don't you see? to live with it; and I seemed to feel that, somehow or other, giving it time and in the long run, it might, it *ought* to, come out on top of the heap. Now that's where, he says, it simply won't do. So must put it – I *have* put it – at the bottom.'

'A very good place, then, for a critical sense!' And Isabel, more placidly now, folded her work. '*If*, that is, you can only keep it there. If it doesn't struggle up again.'

'It can't struggle.' He was still before the fire, looking round at the warm, low room, peaceful in the lamplight, with the hum of the kettle for the ear, with the curtain drawn over the leaded casement, a short moreen curtain artfully chosen by Isabel for the effect of the olden time, its virtue of letting the light within show ruddy to the street. 'It's dead,' he went on; 'I killed it just now.'

He spoke, really, so that she wondered. 'Just now?'

'There in the other place – I strangled it, poor thing, in the dark. If you'll go out and see, there must be blood. Which, indeed,' he added, 'on an altar of sacrifice, is all right. But the place is for ever spattered.'

'I don't want to go out and see.' She rested her locked hands on the needlework folded on her knee, and he knew, with her eyes on him, that a look he had seen before was in her face. 'You're off your head you know, my dear, in a way.' Then, however, more cheeringly: 'It's a good job it hasn't been too late.'

'Too late to get it under?'

'Too late for Them to give you the second chance that I thank God you accept.'

'Yes, if it *had* been –!' And he looked away as through the ruddy curtain and into the chill street. Then he faced her again. 'I've scarcely got over my fright yet. I mean,' he went on, 'for you.'

'And I mean for *you*. Suppose what you had come to announce to me now were that we had *got* the sack. How should I enjoy, do you think, seeing you turn out? Yes, out *there*!' she added as his eyes again moved from their little warm circle to the night of early winter on the other side of the pane, to the rare, quick footsteps, to the closed doors, to the curtains drawn like their own, behind which the small flat town, intrinsically dull, was sitting down to supper.

He stiffened himself as he warmed his back; he held up his head, shaking himself a little as if to shake the stoop out of his shoulders, but he had to allow she was right. 'What would have become of us?'

'What indeed? We should have begged our bread – or I should be taking in washing.'

He was silent a little. 'I'm too old. I should have begun sooner.'

'Oh, God forbid!' she cried.

'The pinch,' he pursued, 'is that I can do nothing else.'

'Nothing whatever!' she agreed with elation.

'Whereas here – if I cultivate it – I perhaps *can* still lie. But I must cultivate it.'

'Oh, you old dear!' And she got up to kiss him.

'I'll do my best,' he said.

7

'Do you remember us?' the gentleman asked and smiled – with the lady beside him smiling too; speaking so much less as an earnest pilgrim or as a tiresome tourist than as an old acquaintance. It was history repeating itself as Gedge had somehow never expected, with almost everything the same except that the evening was now a mild April-end, except that the visitors had put off mourning and showed all their bravery – besides showing, as he doubtless did himself, though so differently, for a little older; except, above all, that – oh, seeing them again suddenly affected him as not a bit the thing he would have thought it. 'We're in England again, and we were near; I've a brother at Oxford with whom we've been spending a day, and we thought we'd come over.' So the young man pleasantly said while our friend took in the queer fact that he must himself seem to them rather coldly to gape. They had come in the same way, at the quiet close; another August had passed, and this was the second spring; the Birthplace, given the hour, was about to suspend operations till the morrow; the last lingerer had gone, and the fancy of the visitors was, once more, for a look round by themselves. This represented surely no greater presumption than the terms on which they had last parted with him seemed to warrant; so that if he did inconsequently stare it was just in fact because he was so supremely far from having forgotten them. But the sight of the pair luckily had a double effect, and the first precipitated the second – the second being really his sudden vision that everything perhaps depended for him on his recognising no complication. He must go straight on, since it was what had for more than a year now so handsomely answered; he must brazen it out consistently, since that only was what his dignity was at last reduced to. He mustn't be afraid in one way any more than he had been in another; besides which it came over him with a force that made him flush that their visit, in its essence, must have been for himself. It was good society again, and *they* were the same. It wasn't for him therefore to behave as if he couldn't meet them.

These deep vibrations, on Gedge's part, were as quick as they were deep; they came in fact all at once, so that his response, his declaration that it was all right – 'Oh, *rather*; the hour doesn't matter for *you*!' – had hung fire but an instant; and when they were within and the door closed behind them, within the twilight of the temple, where, as before, the votive offerings glimmered on the walls, he drew the long breath of one who might, by a self-betrayal, have done something too dreadful. For what had brought them back was not, indubitably, the sentiment of the shrine itself – since he knew their sentiment; but their intelligent interest in the queer case of the priest. Their call was the tribute of curiosity, of sympathy, of a compassion really, as such things went, exquisite – a tribute *to* that queerness which entitled them to the frankest welcome. They had wanted, for the generous wonder of it, to see how he was getting on, how such a man in such a place *could*; and they had doubtless more than half expected to see the door opened by somebody who had succeeded him. Well, somebody *had* – only with a strange equivocation; as they would have, poor things, to make out for themselves, an embarrassment as to which he pitied them. Nothing could have been more odd, but verily it was this troubled vision of their possible bewilderment, and this compunctious view of such a return for their amenity, that practically determined for him his tone. The lapse of the months had but made their name familiar to him; they had on the other occasion inscribed it, among the

thousand names, in the current public register, and he had
since then, for reasons of his own, reasons of feeling, again and
again turned back to it. It was nothing in itself; it told him
nothing – 'Mr and Mrs B.D. Hayes, New York' – one of those
American labels that were just like every other American label
and that were, precisely, the most remarkable thing about
people reduced to achieving an identity in such other ways.
They could be Mr and Mrs B.D. Hayes and yet they could be,
with all presumptions missing – well, what these callers were.
It had quickly enough indeed cleared the situation a little
further that his friends had absolutely, the other time, as it
came back to him, warned him of his original danger, their
anxiety about which had been the last note sounded between
them. What he was afraid of, with this reminiscence, was that,
finding him still safe, they would, the next thing, definitely
congratulate him and perhaps even, no less candidly, ask him
how he had managed. It was with the sense of nipping some
such inquiry in the bud that, losing no time and holding
himself with a firm grip, he began, on the spot, downstairs, to
make plain to them how he had managed. He averted the
question in short by the assurance of his answer. 'Yes, yes, I'm
still here; I suppose it *is* in a manner to one's profit that one
does, such as it is, one's best.' He did his best on the present
occasion, did it with the gravest face he had ever worn and
a soft serenity that was like a large damp sponge passed over
their previous meeting – over everything in it, that is, but the
fact of its pleasantness.

'We stand here, you see, in the old living-room, happily
still to be reconstructed in the mind's eye, in spite of the havoc
of time, which we have fortunately, of late years, been able to
arrest. It was of course rude and humble, but it must have been
snug and quaint, and we have at least the pleasure of knowing

59

that the tradition in respect to the features that do remain is delightfully uninterrupted. Across that threshold He habitually passed; through those low windows, in childhood, He peered out into the world that He was to make so much happier by the gift to it of His genius; over the boards of this floor – that is over *some* of them, for we mustn't be carried away! – his little feet often pattered; and the beams of this ceiling (we must really in some places take care of *our* heads!) he endeavoured, in boyish strife, to jump up and touch. It's not often that in the early home of genius and renown the whole tenor of existence is laid so bare, not often that we are able to retrace, from point to point and from step to step, its connection with objects, with influences – to build it round again with the little solid facts out of which it sprang. This, therefore, I need scarcely remind you, is what makes the small space between these walls – so modest to measurement, so insignificant of aspect – unique on all the earth. *There is nothing like it,*' Morris Gedge went on, insisting as solemnly and softly, for his bewildered hearers, as over a pulpit-edge; 'there is nothing at all like it anywhere in the world. There is nothing, only reflect, for the combination of greatness, and, as we venture to say, of intimacy. You may find elsewhere perhaps absolutely fewer changes, but where shall you find a *Presence* equally diffused, uncontested and undisturbed? Where in particular shall you find, on the part of the abiding spirit, an equally towering eminence? You may find elsewhere eminence of a considerable order, but where shall you find *with* it, don't you see, changes, after all, so few, and the contemporary element caught so, as it were, in the very fact?' His visitors, at first confounded, but gradually spellbound, were still gaping with the universal gape – wondering, he judged, into what strange pleasantry he had been suddenly moved to break out, and yet beginning to see in him an intention beyond a joke, so that they started, at this point, almost jumped, when, by as rapid a transition, he made, toward the old fireplace, a dash that seemed to illustrate, precisely, the act of eager catching. 'It is in this old chimney corner, the quaint inglenook of our ancestors – just there in the far angle, where His little stool was placed, and where, I dare say, if we could look close enough, we should find the hearthstone scraped with His little feet – that we see the inconceivable child gazing into the blaze of the old oaken logs and making out there pictures and stories, see Him conning, with curly bent head, His well-worn hornbook[3], or poring over some scrap of an ancient ballad, some page of some such rudely bound volume of chronicles as lay, we may be sure, in His father's window-seat.'

It was, he even himself felt at this moment, wonderfully done; no auditors, for all his thousands, had ever yet so inspired him. The odd, slightly alarmed shyness in the two faces, as if in a drawing-room, in their 'good society', exactly, some act incongruous, something grazing the indecent, had abruptly been perpetrated, the painful reality of which faltered before coming home – the visible effect on his friends, in fine, wound him up as to the sense that *they* were worth the trick. It came of itself now – he had got it so by heart; but perhaps really it had never come so well, with the staleness so disguised, the interest so renewed and the clerical unction, demanded by the priestly character, so successfully distilled. Mr Hayes of New York had more than once looked at his wife, and Mrs Hayes of New York had more than once looked at her husband – only, up to now, with a stolen glance, with eyes it had not been easy to detach from the remarkable countenance by the aid of which their entertainer held them. At present, however, after an exchange less furtive, they

61

ventured on a sign that they had not been appealed to in vain. 'Charming, charming, Mr Gedge!' Mr Hayes broke out; 'we feel that we've caught you in the mood.'

His wife hastened to assent – it eased the tension. 'It *would* be quite the way; except,' she smiled, 'that you'd be too dangerous. You've really a genius!'

Gedge looked at her hard, but yielding no inch, even though she touched him there at a point of consciousness that quivered. This was the prodigy for him, and had been, the year through – that he did it all, he found, easily, did it better than he had done anything else in his life; with so high and broad an effect, in truth, an inspiration so rich and free, that his poor wife now, literally, had been moved more than once to fresh fear. She had had her bad moments, he knew, after taking the measure of his new direction – moments of readjusted suspicion in which she wondered if he had not simply embraced another, a different perversity. There would be more than one fashion of giving away the show, and wasn't *this* perhaps a question of giving it away by excess? He could dish them by too much romance as well as by too little; she had not hitherto fairly apprehended that there might be too much. It was a way like another, at any rate, of reducing the place to the absurd; which reduction, if he didn't look out, would reduce *them* again to the prospect of the streets, and this time surely without an appeal. It all depended, indeed – he knew she knew that – on how much Grant-Jackson and the others, how much the Body, in a word, would take. He knew she knew what he himself held it would take – that he considered no limit could be drawn to the quantity. They simply wanted it piled up, and so did everybody else; wherefore, if no one reported him, as before, why were They to be uneasy? It was in consequence of idiots brought to reason that he had been dealt with before; but as there was now no form of idiocy that he didn't systematically flatter, goading it on really to its *own* private doom, who was ever to pull the string of the guillotine? The axe was in the air – yes; but in a world gorged to satiety there were no revolutions. And it had been vain for Isabel to ask if the other thunder-growl also hadn't come out of the blue. There was actually proof positive that the winds were now at rest. How could they be more so? – he appealed to the receipts. These were golden days – the show had never so flourished. So he had argued, so he was arguing still – and, it had to be owned, with every appearance in his favour. Yet if he inwardly winced at the tribute to his plausibility rendered by his flushed friends, this was because he felt in it the real ground of his optimism. The charming woman before him acknowledged his 'genius' as he himself had had to do. He had been surprised at his facility until he had grown used to it. Whether or no he had, as a fresh menace to his future, found a new perversity, he had found a vocation much older, evidently, than he had at first been prepared to recognise. He had done himself injustice. He liked to be brave because it came so easy; he could measure it off by the yard. It was in the Birthroom, above all, that he continued to do this, having ushered up his companions without, as he was still more elated to feel, the turn of a hair. She might take it as she liked, but he had had the lucidity – all, that is, for his own safety – to meet without the grace of an answer the homage of her beautiful smile. She took it apparently, and her husband took it, but as a part of his odd humour, and they followed him aloft with faces now a little more responsive to the manner in which, on *that* spot, he would naturally come out. He came out, according to the word of his assured private receipt, 'strong'. He missed a little, in truth, the usual round-eyed question from them – the inveterate artless cue with which, from moment to moment, clustered troops had, for a year, obliged him. Mr and Mrs Hayes were from New York, but it was a little like singing, as he had heard one of his Americans once say about something, to a Boston audience. He did nonetheless what he could, and it was ever his practice to stop still at a certain spot in the room and, after having secured attention by look and gesture, suddenly shoot off. 'Here!'

They always understood, the good people – he could fairly love them now for it; they always said, breathlessly and unanimously, 'There?' and stared down at the designated point quite as if some trace of the grand event were still to be made out. This movement produced, he again looked round. 'Consider it well: *the* spot of earth –!' 'Oh, but it isn't *earth*!' the boldest spirit – there was always a boldest – would generally pipe out. Then the guardian of the Birthplace would be truly superior – as if the unfortunate had figured the Immortal coming up, like a potato, through the soil. 'I'm not suggesting that He was born on the bare ground. He was born *here*!' – with an uncompromising dig of his heel. 'There ought to be a brass, with an inscription, let in.' 'Into the floor?' – it always came. 'Birth and burial: seedtime, summer, autumn!' – that always, with its special, right cadence, thanks to his unfailing spring, came too. 'Why not as well as into the pavement of the church? – you've *seen* our grand old church?' The former of which questions nobody ever answered – abounding, on the other hand, to make up, in relation to the latter. Mr and Mrs Hayes even were at first left dumb by it – not indeed, to do them justice, having uttered the word that produced it. They had uttered no word while he kept the game up, and (though that made it a little more difficult) he could yet stand triumphant before them after he had finished with his flourish. Then it was only that Mr Hayes of New York broke silence.

'Well, if we wanted to see, I think I may say we're quite satisfied. As my wife says, it *would* seem to be your line.' He spoke now, visibly, with more ease, as if a light had come: though he made no joke of it, for a reason that presently appeared. They were coming down the little stair, and it was on the descent that his companion added her word.

'Do you know what we half *did* think –?' And then to her husband: 'Is it dreadful to tell him?' They were in the room below, and the young woman, also relieved, expressed the feeling with gaiety. She smiled, as before, at Morris Gedge, treating him as a person with whom relations were possible, yet remaining just uncertain enough to invoke Mr Hayes's opinion. 'We *have* awfully wanted – from what we had heard.' But she met her husband's graver face; he was not quite out of the wood. At this she was slightly flurried – but she cut it short. 'You must know – don't you? – that, with the crowds who listen to you, we'd have heard.'

He looked from one to the other, and once more again, with force, something came over him. They had kept him in mind, they were neither ashamed nor afraid to show it, and it was positively an interest, on the part of this charming creature and this keen, cautious gentleman, an interest resisting oblivion and surviving separation, that had governed their return. Their other visit had been the brightest thing that had ever happened to him, but this was the gravest; so that at the end of a minute something broke in him and his mask, of itself, fell off. He chucked, as he would have said, consistency; which, in its extinction, left the tears in his eyes. His smile was therefore queer. 'Heard how I'm going it?'

The young man, though still looking at him hard, felt sure, with this, of his own ground. 'Of course, you're tremendously talked about. You've gone round the world.'

'You've heard of me in America?'

'Why, almost of nothing else!'

'That was what made us feel –!' Mrs Hayes contributed.

'That you must see for yourselves?' Again he compared, poor Gedge, their faces. 'Do you mean I excite – a – scandal?'

'Dear no! Admiration. You renew so,' the young man observed, 'the interest.'

'Ah, there it is!' said Gedge with eyes of adventure that seemed to rest beyond the Atlantic.

'They listen, month after month, when they're out here, as you must have seen; and they go home and talk. But they sing your praise.'

Our friend could scarce take it in. 'Over *there*?'

'Over there. I think you must be even in the papers.'

'Without abuse?'

'Oh, we don't abuse everyone.'

Mrs Hayes, in her beauty, it was clear, stretched the point. 'They rave about you.'

'Then they *don't* know?'

'Nobody knows,' the young man declared; 'it wasn't anyone's knowledge, at any rate, that made us uneasy.'

'It was your own? I mean your own sense?'

'Well, call it that. We remembered, and we wondered what had happened. So,' Mr Hayes now frankly laughed, 'we came to see.'

Gedge stared through his film of tears. 'Came from America to see *me*?'

'Oh, a part of the way. But we wouldn't, in England, not have seen you.'

'And now we *have*!' the young woman soothingly added.

Gedge still could only gape at the candour of the tribute. But he tried to meet them – it was what was least poor for him – in their own key. 'Well, how do you like it?'

Mrs Hayes, he thought – if their answer were important – laughed a little nervously. 'Oh, you see.'

Once more he looked from one to the other. 'It's too beastly easy, you know.'

Her husband raised his eyebrows. 'You conceal your art. The emotion – yes; that must be easy; the general tone must flow. But about your facts – you've so many: how do you get *them* through?'

Gedge wondered. 'You think I get too many –?'

At this they were amused together. 'That's just what we came to see!'

'Well, you know, I've felt my way; I've gone step by step; you wouldn't believe how I've tried it on. *This* – where you see me – is where I've come out.' After which, as they said nothing: 'You hadn't thought I *could* come out?'

Again they just waited, but the husband spoke: 'Are you so awfully sure you *are* out?'

Gedge drew himself up in the manner of his moments of emotion, almost conscious even that, with his sloping shoulders, his long lean neck and his nose so prominent in proportion to other matters, he looked the more like a giraffe. It was now at last that he really caught on. 'I *may* be in danger again – and the danger is what has moved you? Oh!' the poor man fairly moaned. His appreciation of it quite weakened him, yet he pulled himself together. 'You've your view of my danger?'

It was wondrous how, with that note definitely sounded, the air was cleared. Lucid Mr Hayes, at the end of a minute, had put the thing in a nutshell. 'I don't know what you'll think of us – for being so beastly curious.'

'I think,' poor Gedge grimaced, 'you're only too beastly kind.'

'It's all your own fault,' his friend returned, 'for presenting us (who are not idiots, say) with so striking a picture of a crisis. At our other visit, you remember,' he smiled, 'you created an anxiety for the opposite reason. Therefore if *this* should again be a crisis for you, you'd really give us the case with an ideal completeness.'

'You make me wish,' said Morris Gedge, 'that it might be one.'

'Well, don't try – for our amusement – to bring one on. I don't see, you know, how you can have much margin. Take care – take care.'

Gedge took it pensively in. 'Yes, that was what you said a year ago. You did me the honour to be uneasy as my wife was.'

Which determined on the young woman's part an immediate question. 'May I ask, then, if Mrs Gedge is now at rest?'

'No; since you do ask. *She* fears, at least, that I go too far; *she* doesn't believe in my margin. You see, we *had* our scare after your visit. They came down.'

His friends were all interest. 'Ah! They came down?'

'Heavy. They brought *me* down. That's *why* –'

'Why you are down?' Mrs Hayes sweetly demanded.

'Ah, but my dear man,' her husband interposed, 'you're not down; you're *up*! You're only up a different tree, but you're up at the tip-top.'

'You mean I take it too high?'

'That's exactly the question,' the young man answered; 'and the possibility, as matching your first danger, is just what we felt we couldn't, if you didn't mind, miss the measure of.'

Gedge looked at him. 'I feel that I know what you at bottom *hoped*.'

'We at bottom "hope", surely, that you're all right.'

'In spite of the fool it makes of everyone?'

Mr Hayes of New York smiled. 'Say *because* of that. We only ask to believe that everyone *is* a fool!'

'Only you haven't been, without reassurance, able to imagine fools of the size that my case demands?' And Gedge had a pause, while, as if on the chance of some proof, his companion waited. 'Well, I won't pretend to you that your anxiety hasn't made me, doesn't threaten to make me, a bit nervous; though I don't quite understand it if, as you say, people but rave about me.'

'Oh, *that* report was from the other side; people in our country so very easily rave. You've seen small children laugh to shrieks when tickled in a new place. So there are amiable millions with us who are but small children. They perpetually present new places for the tickler. What we've seen in further lights,' Mr Hayes good-humouredly pursued, 'is your people *here* – the Committee, the Board, or whatever the powers to whom you're responsible.'

'Call them my friend Grant-Jackson then – my original backer, though I admit, for that reason, perhaps my most formidable critic. It's with him, practically, I deal; or rather it's by him I'm dealt with – *was* dealt with before. I stand or fall by him. But he has given me my head.'

'Mayn't he then want you,' Mrs Hayes enquired, 'just to show as flagrantly running away?'

'Of course – I see what you mean. I'm riding, blindly, for a fall, and They're watching (to be tender of me!) for the smash that may come of itself. It's Machiavellic – but everything's possible. And what did you just now mean,' Gedge asked – 'especially if you've only heard of my prosperity – by your "further lights"?'

His friends for an instant looked embarrassed, but Mr Hayes came to the point. 'We've heard of your prosperity, but we've also, remember, within a few minutes, heard *you*.'

'I was determined you *should*,' said Gedge. 'I'm good then – but I overdo?' His strained grin was still sceptical.

Thus challenged, at any rate, his visitor pronounced. 'Well, if you don't; if at the end of six months more it's clear that you haven't overdone; then, *then* –'

'Then what?'

'Then it's great.'

'But it *is* great – greater than anything of the sort ever was. I overdo, thank goodness, yes; or I would if it were a thing you *could*.'

'Oh, well, if there's *proof* that you can't –!' With which, and an expressive gesture, Mr Hayes threw up his fears.

His wife, however, for a moment, seemed unable to let them go. 'Don't They want then *any* truth? – none even for the mere look of it?'

'The look of it,' said Morris Gedge, 'is what I give!'

It made them, the others, exchange a look of their own. Then she smiled. 'Oh, well, if they think so –!'

'You at least don't? You're like my wife – which indeed, I remember,' Gedge added, 'is a similarity I expressed a year ago the wish for! At any rate I frighten *her*.'

The young husband, with an 'Ah, wives are terrible!' smoothed it over, and their visit would have failed of further excuse had not, at this instant, a movement at the other end of the room suddenly engaged them. The evening had so nearly closed in, though Gedge, in the course of their talk, had lighted the lamp nearest them, that they had not distinguished, in connection with the opening of the door of communication to the warden's lodge, the appearance of another person, an eager woman, who, in her impatience, had barely paused before advancing. Mrs Gedge – her identity took but a few seconds to become vivid – was upon them, and she had not been too late for Mr Hayes's last remark. Gedge saw at once that she had come with news; no need even, for that certitude, of her quick retort to the words in the air – 'You may say as well, sir, that they're often, poor wives, terrified!' She knew nothing of the friends whom, at so unnatural an hour, he was showing about; but there was no livelier sign for him that this didn't matter than the possibility with which she intensely charged her 'Grant-Jackson, to see you at once!' – letting it, so to speak, fly in his face.

'He has been with you?'

'Only a minute – he's there. But it's you he wants to see.'

He looked at the others. 'And what does he want, dear?'

'God knows! There it is. It's his horrid hour – it *was* that other time.'

She had nervously turned to the others, overflowing to them, in her dismay, for all their strangeness – quite, as he said to himself, like a woman of the people. She was the bare-headed goodwife talking in the street about the row in the house, and it was in this character that he instantly introduced her: 'My dear doubting wife, who will do her best to entertain you while I wait upon our friend.' And he explained to her as he could his now protesting companions – 'Mr and Mrs Hayes of New York, who have been here before.' He knew, without knowing why, that her announcement chilled him; he failed at least to see why it should chill him so much. His good friends had themselves been visibly affected by it, and heaven knew that the depths of brooding fancy in him were easily stirred by contact. If they had wanted a crisis they accordingly had found one, albeit they had already asked leave to retire before it. This he wouldn't have. 'Ah no, you must really see!'

71

'But we shan't be able to bear it, you know,' said the young woman, 'if it *is* to turn you out.'

Her crudity attested her sincerity, and it was the latter, doubtless, that instantly held Mrs Gedge. 'It *is* to turn us out.'

'Has he told you that, madam?' Mr Hayes enquired of her – it being wondrous how the breath of doom had drawn them together.

'No, not told me; but there's something in him there – I mean in his awful manner – that matches too well with other things. We've seen,' said the poor pale lady, 'other things enough.'

The young woman almost clutched her. 'Is his manner very awful?'

'It's simply the manner,' Gedge interposed, 'of a very great man.'

'Well, very great men,' said his wife, 'are very awful things.'

'It's exactly,' he laughed, 'what we're finding out! But I mustn't keep him waiting. Our friends here,' he went on, 'are directly interested. You mustn't, mind you, let them go until we know.'

Mr Hayes, however, held him; he found himself stayed. 'We're so directly interested that I want you to understand this. If anything happens –'

'Yes?' said Gedge, all gentle as he faltered.

'Well, *we* must set you up.'

Mrs Hayes quickly abounded. 'Oh, *do* come to us!'

Again he could but look at them. They were really wonderful folk. And but Mr and Mrs Hayes! It affected even Isabel, through her alarm; though the balm, in a manner, seemed to foretell the wound. He had reached the threshold of his own quarters; he stood there as at the door of the chamber of judgement. But he laughed; at least he could be gallant in going up for sentence. 'Very good then – I'll come to you!'

This was very well, but it didn't prevent his heart, a minute later, at the end of the passage, from thumping with beats he could count. He had paused again before going in; on the other side of this second door his poor future was to be let loose at him. It was broken, at best, and spiritless, but wasn't Grant-Jackson there, like a beast-tamer in a cage, all tights and spangles and circus attitudes, to give it a cut with the smart official whip and make it spring at him? It was during this moment that he fully measured the effect for his nerves of the impression made on his so oddly earnest friends – whose earnestness he in fact, in the spasm of this last effort, came within an ace of resenting. They had upset him by contact; he was afraid, literally, of meeting his doom on his knees; it wouldn't have taken much more, he absolutely felt, to make him approach with his fore-head in the dust the great man whose wrath was to be averted. Mr and Mrs Hayes of New York had brought tears to his eyes; but was it to be reserved for Grant-Jackson to make him cry like a baby? He wished, yes, while he palpitated, that Mr and Mrs Hayes of New York hadn't had such an eccentricity of interest, for it seemed somehow to come from *them* that he was going so fast to pieces. Before he turned the knob of the door, how-ever, he had another queer instant; making out that it had been, strictly, his case that was interesting, his funny power, however accidental, to show as in a picture the attitude of others – not his poor, dingy personality. It was this latter quantity, nonetheless, that was marching to execution. It is to our friend's credit that he *believed*, as he prepared to turn the knob, that he was going to be hanged; and it is certainly not less to his credit that his wife, on the chance, had his supreme thought. Here it was that – possibly with his last articulate breath – he thanked his stars, such as they were, for Mr and Mrs Hayes of New York. At least they would take care of her.

They were doing that certainly with some success when, ten minutes later, he returned to them. She sat between them in the beautified Birthplace, and he couldn't have been sure afterwards that each wasn't holding her hand. The three together, at any rate, had the effect of recalling to him – it was too whimsical – some picture, a sentimental print, seen and admired in his youth, a 'Waiting for the Verdict', a 'Counting the Hours', or something of that sort; humble respectability in suspense about humble innocence. He didn't know how he himself looked, and he didn't care; the great thing was that he wasn't crying – though he might have been; the glitter in his eyes was assuredly dry, though that there was a glitter, or something slightly to bewilder, the faces of the others, as they rose to meet him, sufficiently proved. His wife's eyes pierced his own, but it was Mrs Hayes of New York who spoke. '*Was* it then for that –?'

He only looked at them at first – he felt he might now enjoy it. 'Yes, it was for "that". I mean it was about the way I've been going on. He came to speak of it.'

'And he's gone?' Mr Hayes permitted himself to enquire.

'He's gone.'

'It's over?' Isabel hoarsely asked.

'It's over.'

'Then we go?'

This it was that he enjoyed. 'No, my dear; we stay.'

There was fairly a triple gasp; relief took time to operate. 'Then why did he come?'

'In the fullness of his kind heart and of *Their* discussed and decreed satisfaction. To express Their sense –!'

Mr Hayes broke into a laugh, but his wife wanted to know. 'Of the grand work you're doing?'

'Of the way I polish it off. They're most handsome about it. The receipts, it appears, speak –'

He was nursing his effect; Isabel intently watched him, and the others hung on his lips. 'Yes, speak –?'

'Well, volumes. They tell the truth.'

At this Mr Hayes laughed again. 'Oh, *they* at least do?'

Near him thus, once more, Gedge knew their intelligence as one – which was so good a consciousness to get back that his tension now relaxed as by the snap of a spring and he felt his old face at ease. 'So you can't say,' he continued, 'that we don't want it.'

'I bow to it,' the young man smiled. 'It's what I said then. It's *great*.'

'It's great,' said Morris Gedge. 'It couldn't be greater.'

His wife still watched him; her irony hung behind. 'Then we're just as we were?'

'No, not as we were.'

She jumped at it. 'Better?'

'Better. They give us a rise.'

'Of income?'

'Of our sweet little stipend – by a vote of the Committee. That's what, as Chairman, he came to announce.'

The very echoes of the Birthplace were themselves, for the instant, hushed; the warden's three companions showed, in the conscious air, a struggle for their own breath. But Isabel, with almost a shriek, was the first to recover hers. 'They double us?'

'Well – call it that. "In recognition." There you are.' Isabel uttered another sound – but this time inarticulate; partly because Mrs Hayes of New York had already jumped at her to kiss her. Mr Hayes meanwhile, as with too much to say, but put out his hand, which our friend took in silence. So Gedge had the last word. 'And there *you* are!'

The Private Life

We talked of London, face to face with a great bristling, primeval glacier. The hour and the scene were one of those impressions which make up a little, in Switzerland, for the modern indignity of travel – the promiscuities and vulgarities, the station and the hotel, the gregarious patience, the struggle for a scrappy attention, the reduction to a numbered state. The high valley was pink with the mountain rose, the cool air as fresh as if the world were young. There was a faint flush of afternoon on undiminished snows, and the fraternizing tinkle of the unseen cattle came to us with a cropped and sun-warmed odour. The balconied inn stood on the very neck of the sweetest pass in the Oberland, and for a week we had had company and weather. This was felt to be great luck, for one would have made up for the other had either been bad.

The weather certainly would have made up for the company; but it was not subjected to this tax, for we had by a happy chance the *fleur des pois*[4]: Lord and Lady Mellifont, Clare Vawdrey, the greatest (in the opinion of many) of our literary glories, and Blanche Adney, the greatest (in the opinion of all) of our theatrical. I mention these first, because they were just the people whom in London, at that time, people tried to 'get'. People endeavoured to 'book' them six weeks ahead, yet on this occasion we had come in for them, we had all come in for each other, without the least wire-pulling. A turn of the game had pitched us together, the last of August, and we recognised our luck by remaining so, under protection of the barometer. When the golden days were over – that would come soon enough – we should wind down opposite sides of the pass and disappear over the crest of surrounding heights. We were of the same general communion, we participated in the same miscellaneous publicity. We met, in London, with irregular frequency; we were more or less governed by the laws and the language, the traditions and the shibboleths of the same dense social state. I think all of us, even the ladies, 'did' something, though we pretended we didn't when it was mentioned. Such things are not mentioned indeed in London, but it was our innocent pleasure to be different here. There had to be some way to show the difference, inasmuch as we were under the impression that this was our annual holiday. We felt at any rate that the conditions were more human than in London, or that at least we ourselves were. We were frank about this, we talked about it: it was what we were talking about as we looked at the flushing glacier, just as someone called attention to the prolonged absence of Lord Mellifont and Mrs Adney. We were seated on the terrace of the inn, where there were benches and little tables, and those of us who were most bent on proving that we had returned to nature were, in the queer Germanic fashion, having coffee before meat.

The remark about the absence of our two companions was not taken up, not even by Lady Mellifont, not even by little Adney, the fond composer; for it had been dropped only in the briefest intermission of Clare Vawdrey's talk. (This celebrity was 'Clarence' only on the title-page.) It was just that revelation of our being after all human that was his theme. He asked the company whether, candidly, everyone hadn't been tempted to say to everyone else: 'I had no idea you were really so nice.' I had had, for my part, an idea that he was, and even a good deal nicer, but that was too complicated to go into then; besides it is exactly my story. There was a general understanding among us that when Vawdrey talked we should be silent, and not, oddly enough, because he at all expected it. He didn't, for of all abundant talkers he was the most unconscious, the least greedy and professional. It was rather the religion of the host, of the hostess, that prevailed among us:

it was their own idea, but they always looked for a listening circle when the great novelist dined with them. On the occasion I allude to there was probably no one present with whom, in London, he had not dined, and we felt the force of this habit. He had dined even with me; and on the evening of that dinner, as on this Alpine afternoon, I had been at no pains to hold my tongue, absorbed as I inveterately was in a study of the question which always rose before me, to such a height, in his fair, square, strong stature.

This question was all the more tormenting that he never suspected himself (I am sure) of imposing it, any more than he had ever observed that every day of his life everyone listened to him at dinner. He used to be called 'subjective' in the weekly papers, but in society no distinguished man could have been less so. He never talked about himself; and this was a topic on which, though it would have been tremendously worthy of him, he apparently never even reflected. He had his hours and his habits, his tailor and his hatter, his hygiene and his particular wine, but all these things together never made up an attitude. Yet they constituted the only attitude he ever adopted, and it was easy for him to refer to our being 'nicer' abroad than at home. *He* was exempt from variations, and not a shade either less or more nice in one place than in another. He differed from other people, but never from himself (save in the extraordinary sense which I will presently explain), and struck me as having neither moods nor sensibilities nor preferences. He might have been always in the same company, so far as he recognised any influence from age or condition or sex: he addressed himself to women exactly as he addressed himself to men, and gossiped with all men alike, talking no better to clever folk than to dull. I used to feel a despair at his way of liking one subject – so far as I could tell – precisely as much as another: there were some I hated so myself. I never found him anything but loud and cheerful and copious, and I never heard him utter a paradox or express a shade or play with an idea. That fancy about our being 'human' was, in his conversation, quite an exceptional flight. His opinions were sound and second-rate, and of his perceptions it was too mystifying to think. I envied him his magnificent health.

Vawdrey had marched, with his even pace and his perfectly good conscience, into the flat country of anecdote, where stories are visible from afar like windmills and signposts; but I observed after a little that Lady Mellifont's attention wandered. I happened to be sitting next her. I noticed that her eyes rambled a little anxiously over the lower slopes of the mountains. At last, after looking at her watch, she said to me: 'Do you know where they went?'

'Do you mean Mrs Adney and Lord Mellifont?'

'Lord Mellifont and Mrs Adney.' Her ladyship's speech seemed – unconsciously indeed – to *correct* me, but it didn't occur to me that this was because she was jealous. I imputed to her no such vulgar sentiment: in the first place, because I liked her, and in the second because it would always occur to one quickly that it was right, in any connection, to put Lord Mellifont first. He was first – extraordinarily first. I don't say greatest or wisest or most renowned, but essentially at the top of the list and the head of the table. That is a position by itself, and his wife was naturally accustomed to see him in it. My phrase had sounded as if Mrs Adney had taken him; but it was not possible for him to be taken – he only took. No one, in the nature of things, could know this better than Lady Mellifont. I had originally been rather afraid of her, thinking her, with her stiff silences and the extreme blackness of almost everything that made up her person, somewhat hard, even a little saturnine. Her paleness seemed slightly grey, and her glossy black hair metallic, like the brooches and bands and combs with which it was inveterately adorned. She was in perpetual mourning, and wore numberless ornaments of jet and onyx, a thousand clicking chains and bugles and beads. I had heard Mrs Adney call her the queen of night, and the term was descriptive if you understood that the night was cloudy. She had a secret, and if you didn't find it out as you knew her better you at least perceived that she was gentle and unaffected and limited, and also rather submissively sad. She was like a woman with a painless malady. I told her that I had merely seen her husband and his companion stroll down the glen together about an hour before, and suggested that Mr Adney would perhaps know something of their intentions.

Vincent Adney, who, though he was fifty years old, looked like a good little boy on whom it had been impressed that children should not talk before company, acquitted himself with remarkable simplicity and taste of the position of husband of a great exponent of comedy. When all was said about her making it easy for him, one couldn't help admiring the charmed affection with which he took everything for granted. It is difficult for a husband who is not on the stage, or at least in the theatre, to be graceful about a wife who is; but Adney was more than graceful – he was exquisite, he was inspired. He set his beloved to music; and you remember how genuine his music could be – the only English compositions I ever saw a foreigner take an interest in. His wife was in them, somewhere, always; they were like a free, rich translation of the impression she produced. She seemed, as one listened, to pass laughing, with loosened hair, across the scene. He had been only a little fiddler at her theatre, always in his place during the acts; but she had made him something rare and misunderstood.

Their superiority had become a kind of partnership, and their happiness was a part of the happiness of their friends. Adney's one discomfort was that he couldn't write a play for his wife, and the only way he meddled with her affairs was by asking impossible people if *they* couldn't.

Lady Mellifont, after looking across at him a moment, remarked to me that she would rather not put any question to him. She added the next minute: 'I had rather people shouldn't see I'm nervous.'

'Are you nervous?'

'I always become so if my husband is away from me for any time.'

'Do you imagine something has happened to him?'

'Yes, always. Of course I'm used to it.'

'Do you mean his tumbling over precipices – that sort of thing?'

'I don't know exactly what it is: it's the general sense that he'll never come back.'

She said so much and kept back so much that the only way to treat the condition she referred to seemed the jocular. 'Surely he'll never forsake you!' I laughed.

She looked at the ground a moment. 'Oh, at bottom I'm easy.'

'Nothing can ever happen to a man so accomplished, so infallible, so armed at all points,' I went on, encouragingly.

'Oh, you don't know how he's armed!' she exclaimed, with such an odd quaver that I could account for it only by her being nervous. This idea was confirmed by her moving just afterwards, changing her seat rather pointlessly, not as if to cut our conversation short, but because she was in a fidget. I couldn't know what was the matter with her, but I was presently relieved to see Mrs Adney come toward us. She had in her hand a big bunch of wild flowers, but she was not closely attended by Lord Mellifont. I quickly saw, however, that she had no disaster to announce; yet as I knew there was a question Lady Mellifont would like to hear answered, but did not wish to ask, I expressed to her immediately the hope that his lordship had not remained in a crevasse.

'Oh, no; he left me but three minutes ago. He has gone into the house.' Blanche Adney rested her eyes on mine an instant – a mode of intercourse to which no man, for himself, could ever object. The interest, on this occasion, was quickened by the particular thing the eyes happened to say. What they usually said was only: 'Oh, yes, I'm charming, I know, but don't make a fuss about it. I only want a new part – I do, I do!' At present they added, dimly, surreptitiously, and of course sweetly – for that was the way they did everything: 'It's all right, but something did happen. Perhaps I'll tell you later.' She turned to Lady Mellifont, and the transition to simple gaiety suggested her mastery of her profession. 'I've brought him safe. We had a charming walk.'

'I'm so very glad,' returned Lady Mellifont, with her faint smile; continuing vaguely, as she got up: 'He must have gone to dress for dinner. Isn't it rather near?' She moved away, to the hotel, in her leave-taking, simplifying fashion, and the rest of us, at the mention of dinner, looked at each other's watches, as if to shift the responsibility of such grossness. The head-waiter, essentially, like all head-waiters, a man of the world, allowed us hours and places of our own, so that in the evening, apart under the lamp, we formed a compact, an indulged little circle. But it was only the Mellifonts who 'dressed' and as to whom it was recognised that they naturally *would* dress: she in exactly the same manner as on any other evening of her ceremonious existence (she was not a woman whose habits could take account of anything so mutable as fitness); and he, on the other hand, with remarkable adjustment and suitability. He was almost as much a man of the world as the head-waiter, and spoke almost as many languages; but he abstained from courting a comparison of dress-coats and white waistcoats, analysing the occasion in a much finer way – into black velvet and blue velvet and brown velvet, for instance, into delicate harmonies of necktie and subtle informalities of shirt. He had a costume for every function and a moral for every costume; and his functions and costumes and morals were ever a part of the amusement of life – a part at any rate of its beauty and romance – for an immense circle of spectators. For his particular friends indeed these things were more than an amusement; they were a topic, a social support and of course, in addition, a subject of perpetual suspense. If his wife had not been present before dinner they were what the rest of us probably would have been putting our heads together about.

Clare Vawdrey had a fund of anecdote on the whole question: he had known Lord Mellifont almost from the beginning. It was a peculiarity of this nobleman that there could be no conversation about him that didn't instantly take the form of anecdote, and a still further distinction that there could apparently be no anecdote that was not on the whole to his honour. If he had come into a room at any moment, people might have said frankly: 'Of course we were telling stories about you!' As consciences go, in London, the general conscience would have been good. Moreover it would have been impossible to imagine his taking such a tribute otherwise than amiably, for he was always as unperturbed as an actor with the right cue. He had never in his life needed the prompter – his very embarrassments had been rehearsed. For myself, when he was talked about I always had an odd impression that we were speaking of the dead – it was with that peculiar accumulation of relish. His reputation was a kind of gilded obelisk, as if he had been buried beneath it; the body of legend and reminiscence of which he was to be the subject had crystallized in advance.

This ambiguity sprang, I suppose, from the fact that the mere sound of his name and air of his person, the general expectation he created, were, somehow, too exalted to be verified. The experience of his urbanity always came later; the prefigurement, the legend paled before the reality. I remember that on the evening I refer to the reality was particularly operative. The handsomest man of his period could never have looked better, and he sat among us like a bland conductor controlling by an harmonious play of arm an orchestra still a little rough. He directed the conversation by gestures as irresistible as they were vague; one felt as if without him it wouldn't have had anything to call a tone. This was essentially what he contributed to any occasion – what he contributed above all to English public life. He pervaded it, he coloured it, he embellished it, and without him it would scarcely have had a vocabulary. Certainly it would not have had a style; for a style was what it had in having Lord Mellifont. He *was* a style. I was freshly struck with it as, in the *salle à manger*[5] of the little Swiss inn, we resigned ourselves to inevitable veal. Confronted with his form (I must parenthesize that it was not confronted much), Clare Vawdrey's talk suggested the reporter contrasted with the bard. It was interesting to watch the shock of characters from which, of an evening, so much would be expected. There was however no concussion – it was all muffled and minimized in Lord Mellifont's tact. It was rudimentary with him to find the solution of such a problem in playing the host, assuming responsibilities which carried with them their sacrifice. He had indeed never been a guest in his life; he was the host, the patron, the moderator at every board. If there was a defect in his manner (and I suggest it under my breath), it was that he had a little more art than any conjunction – even the most complicated – could possibly require. At any rate one made one's reflections in noticing how the accomplished peer handled the situation and how the sturdy man of letters was unconscious that the situation (and least of all he himself as part of it), was handled. Lord Mellifont poured forth treasures of tact, and Clare Vawdrey never dreamed he was doing it.

Vawdrey had no suspicion of any such precaution even when Blanche Adney asked him if he saw yet their third act – an inquiry into which she introduced a subtlety of her own. She had a theory that he was to write her a play and that the heroine, if he would only do his duty, would be the part for which she had immemorially longed. She was forty years old (this could be no secret to those who had admired her from the first), and she could now reach out her hand and touch her uttermost goal. This gave a kind of tragic passion – perfect actress of comedy as she was – to her desire not to miss the great thing. The years had passed, and still she had missed it; none of the things she had done was the thing she had dreamed of, so that at present there was no more time to lose. This was the canker in the rose, the ache beneath the smile. It made her touching – made her sadness even sweeter than her laughter. She had done the old English and the new French, and had charmed her generation; but she was haunted by the vision of a bigger chance, of something truer to the conditions that lay near her. She was tired of Sheridan and she hated Bowdler; she called for a canvas of a finer grain. The worst of it, to my sense, was that she would never extract her modern comedy from the great mature novelist, who was as incapable of producing it as he was of threading a needle. She coddled him, she talked to him, she made love to him, as she frankly proclaimed; but she dwelt in illusions – she would have to live and die with Bowdler.

It is difficult to be cursory over this charming woman, who was beautiful without beauty and complete with a dozen deficiencies. The perspective of the stage made her over, and in society she was like the model off the pedestal. She was the picture walking about, which to the artless social mind was a perpetual surprise – a miracle. People thought she told them the secrets of the pictorial nature, in return for which they gave her relaxation and tea. She told them nothing and she drank the tea; but they had, all the same, the best of the bargain. Vawdrey was really at work on a play; but if he had begun it because he liked her I think he let it drag for the same reason. He secretly felt the atrocious difficulty – knew that from his hand the finished piece would have received no active life. At the same time nothing could be more agreeable than to have such a question open with Blanche Adney, and from time to time he put something very good into the play. If he deceived Mrs Adney it was only because in her despair she was determined to be deceived. To her question about their third act he replied that, before dinner, he had written a magnificent passage.

'Before dinner?' I said. 'Why, *cher maître*[6], before dinner you were holding us all spellbound on the terrace.'

My words were a joke, because I thought his had been; but for the first time that I could remember I perceived a certain confusion in his face. He looked at me hard, throwing back his head quickly, the least bit like a horse who has been pulled up short. 'Oh, it was before that,' he replied, naturally enough.

'Before that you were playing billiards with *me*,' Lord Mellifont intimated.

'Then it must have been yesterday,' said Vawdrey.

But he was in a tight place. 'You told me this morning you did nothing yesterday,' the actress objected.

'I don't think I really know when I do things.' Vawdrey looked vaguely, without helping himself, at a dish that was offered him.

'It's enough if we know,' smiled Lord Mellifont.

'I don't believe you've written a line,' said Blanche Adney.

'I think I could repeat you the scene.' Vawdrey helped himself to *haricots verts*[7].

'Oh, do – oh, do!' two or three of us cried.

'After dinner, in the salon; it will be an immense *régal*,' Lord Mellifont declared.

'I'm not sure, but I'll try,' Vawdrey went on.

'Oh, you lovely man!' exclaimed the actress, who was practising Americanisms, being resigned even to an American comedy.

'But there must be this condition,' said Vawdrey: 'you must make your husband play.'

'Play while you're reading? Never!'

'I've too much vanity,' said Adney.

Lord Mellifont distinguished him. 'You must give us the overture, before the curtain rises. That's a peculiarly delightful moment.'

'I shan't read – I shall just speak,' said Vawdrey.

'Better still, let me go and get your manuscript,' the actress suggested.

Vawdrey replied that the manuscript didn't matter; but an hour later, in the salon, we wished he might have had it. We sat expectant, still under the spell of Adney's violin. His wife, in the foreground, on an ottoman, was all impatience and profile, and Lord Mellifont, in *the* chair – it was always the chair, Lord Mellifont's – made our grateful little group feel like a social science congress or a distribution of prizes. Suddenly, instead of beginning, our tame lion began to roar out of tune – he had clean forgotten every word. He was very sorry, but the lines absolutely wouldn't come to him; he was utterly ashamed, but his memory was a blank. He didn't look in the least ashamed – Vawdrey had never looked ashamed in his life; he was only imperturbably and merrily natural. He protested that he had never expected to make such a fool of himself, but we felt that this wouldn't prevent the incident from taking its place among his jolliest reminiscences. It was only we who were humiliated, as if he had played us a premeditated trick. This was an occasion, if ever, for Lord Mellifont's tact, which descended on us all like balm: he told us, in his charming artistic way, his way of bridging over arid intervals (he had a *débit* – there was nothing to approach it in England – like the actors of the *Comédie Française*), of his own collapse on a momentous occasion, the delivery of an address to a mighty multitude, when, finding he had forgotten his memoranda, he fumbled, on the terrible platform, the cynosure of every eye, fumbled vainly in irreproachable pockets for indispensable notes. But the point of his story was finer than that of Vawdrey's pleasantry; for he sketched with a few light gestures the brilliancy of a performance which had risen superior to embarrassment, had resolved itself, we were left to divine, into an effort recognised at the moment as not absolutely a blot on what the public was so good as to call his reputation.

'Play up – play up!' cried Blanche Adney, tapping her husband and remembering how, on the stage, a contretemps is always drowned in music. Adney threw himself upon his fiddle, and I said to Clare Vawdrey that his mistake could easily be corrected by his sending for the manuscript. If he would tell me where it was I would immediately fetch it from his room. To this he replied: 'My dear fellow, I'm afraid there *is* no manuscript.'

'Then you've not written anything?'

'I'll write it tomorrow.'

'Ah, you trifle with us,' I said, in much mystification.

Vawdrey hesitated an instant. 'If there *is* anything, you'll find it on my table.'

At this moment one of the others spoke to him, and Lady Mellifont remarked audibly, as if to correct gently our want of consideration, that Mr Adney was playing something very beautiful. I had noticed before that she appeared extremely fond of music; she always listened to it in a hushed transport. Vawdrey's attention was drawn away, but it didn't seem to me that the words he had just dropped constituted a definite permission to go to his room. Moreover I wanted to speak to Blanche Adney; I had something to ask her. I had to await my chance, however, as we remained silent awhile for her husband, after which the conversation became general. It was our habit to go to bed early, but there was still a little of the evening left. Before it quite waned I found an opportunity to tell the actress that Vawdrey had given me leave to put my hand on his manuscript. She adjured me, by all I held sacred, to bring it immediately, to give it to her; and her insistence was proof against my suggestion that it would now be too late for him to begin to read: besides which the charm was broken – the others wouldn't care. It was not too late for *her* to begin; therefore I was to possess myself, without more delay, of the precious pages. I told her she should be obeyed in a moment, but I wanted her first to satisfy my just curiosity.

What had happened before dinner, while she was on the hills with Lord Mellifont?

'How do you know anything happened?'

'I saw it in your face when you came back.'

'And they call me an actress!' cried Mrs Adney.

'What do they call *me*?' I enquired.

'You're a searcher of hearts – that frivolous thing an observer.'

'I wish you'd let an observer write you a play!' I broke out.

'People don't care for what you write: you'd break any run of luck.'

'Well, I see plays all round me,' I declared; 'the air is full of them tonight.'

'The air? Thank you for nothing! I only wish my table-drawers were.'

'Did he make love to you on the glacier?' I went on.

She stared; then broke into the graduated ecstasy of her laugh. 'Lord Mellifont, poor dear? What a funny place! It would indeed be the place for *our* love!'

'Did he fall into a crevasse?' I continued.

Blanche Adney looked at me again as she had done for an instant when she came up, before dinner, with her hands full of flowers. 'I don't know into what he fell. I'll tell you tomorrow.'

'He did come down, then?'

'Perhaps he went up,' she laughed. 'It's really strange.'

'All the more reason you should tell me tonight.'

'I must think it over; I must puzzle it out.'

'Oh, if you want conundrums I'll throw in another,' I said. 'What's the matter with the master?'

'The master of what?'

'Of every form of dissimulation. Vawdrey hasn't written a line.'

'Go and get his papers and we'll see.'

'I don't like to expose him,' I said.

'Why not, if I expose Lord Mellifont?'

'Oh, I'd do anything for that,' I conceded. 'But why should Vawdrey have made a false statement? It's very curious.'

'It's very curious,' Blanche Adney repeated, with a musing air and her eyes on Lord Mellifont. Then, rousing herself, she added: 'Go and look in his room.'

'In Lord Mellifont's?'

She turned to me quickly. '*That* would be a way!'

'A way to what?'

'To find out – to find out!' She spoke gaily and excitedly, but suddenly checked herself. 'We're talking nonsense,' she said.

'We're mixing things up, but I'm struck with your idea. Get Lady Mellifont to let you.'

'Oh, *she* has looked!' Mrs Adney murmured, with the oddest dramatic expression. Then, after a movement of her beautiful uplifted hand, as if to brush away a fantastic vision, she exclaimed imperiously: 'Bring me the scene – bring me the scene!'

'I go for it,' I answered; 'but don't tell me I can't write a play.'

She left me, but my errand was arrested by the approach of a lady who had produced a birthday-book – we had been threatened with it for several evenings – and who did me the honour to solicit my autograph. She had been asking the others, and she couldn't decently leave me out. I could usually remember my name, but it always took me some time to recall my date, and even when I had done so I was never very sure. I hesitated between two days and I remarked to my petitioner that I would sign on both if it would give her any satisfaction. She said that surely I had been born only once; and I replied of course that on the day I made her acquaintance I had been born again. I mention the feeble joke only to show that, with the obligatory inspection of the other autographs, we gave some minutes to this transaction. The lady departed with her book, and then I became aware that the company had dispersed. I was alone in the little salon that had been appropriated to our use. My first impression was one of disappointment: if Vawdrey had gone to bed I didn't wish to disturb him. While I hesitated, however, I recognised that Vawdrey had not gone to bed. A window was open, and the sound of voices outside came in to me: Blanche was on the terrace with her dramatist, and they were talking about the stars. I went to the window for a glimpse – the Alpine night was splendid. My friends had stepped out together; the actress had picked up a cloak; she looked as I had seen her look in the wing of the theatre. They were silent awhile, and I heard the roar of a neighbouring torrent. I turned back into the room, and its quiet lamplight gave me an idea. Our companions had dispersed – it was late for a pastoral country – and we three should have the place to ourselves. Clare Vawdrey had written his scene – it was magnificent; and his reading it to us there, at such an hour, would be an episode intensely memorable. I would bring down his manuscript and meet the two with it as they came in.

I quitted the salon for this purpose; I had been in Vawdrey's room and knew it was on the second floor, the last in a long corridor. A minute later my hand was on the knob of his door, which I naturally pushed open without knocking. It was equally natural that in the absence of its occupant the room should be dark; the more so as, the end of the corridor being at that hour unlighted, the obscurity was not imme-diately diminished by the opening of the door. I was only aware at first that I had made no mistake and that, the window-curtains not being drawn, I was confronted with a couple of vague starlighted apertures. Their aid, however, was not sufficient to enable me to find what I had come for, and my hand, in my pocket, was already on the little box of matches that I always carried for cigarettes. Suddenly I withdrew it with a start, uttering an ejaculation, an apology. I had entered the wrong room; a glance prolonged for three seconds showed me a figure seated at a table near one of the windows – a figure I had at first taken for a travelling-rug thrown over a chair. I retreated, with a sense of intrusion; but as I did so I became aware, more rapidly than it takes me to express it, in the first place that this was Vawdrey's room and in the second that, most singularly, Vawdrey himself sat before me. Checking myself on the threshold I had a momentary feeling of bewilderment, but before I knew it I had exclaimed: 'Hullo! is that you, Vawdrey?'

He neither turned nor answered me, but my question received an immediate and practical reply in the opening of a door on the other side of the passage. A servant, with a candle, had come out of the opposite room, and in this flitting illumination I definitely recognised the man whom, an instant before, I had to the best of my belief left below in conversation with Mrs Adney. His back was half turned to me, and he bent over the table in the attitude of writing, but I was conscious that I was in no sort of error about his identity. 'I beg your pardon – I thought you were downstairs,' I said; and as the personage gave no sign of hearing me I added: 'If you're busy I won't disturb you.' I backed out, closing the door – I had been in the place, I suppose, less than a minute. I had a sense of mystification, which however deepened infinitely the next instant. I stood there with my hand still on the knob of the door, overtaken by the oddest impression of my life. Vawdrey was at his table, writing, and it was a very natural place for him to be; but why was he writing in the dark and why hadn't he answered me? I waited a few seconds for the sound of some movement, to see if he wouldn't rouse himself from his abstraction – a fit conceivable in a great writer – and call out: 'Oh, my dear fellow, is it you?' But I heard only the stillness, I felt only the starlighted dusk of the room, with the unexpected presence it enclosed. I turned away, slowly retracing my steps, and came confusedly downstairs. The lamp was still burning in the salon, but the room was empty. I passed round to the door of the hotel and stepped out. Empty too was the terrace. Blanche Adney and the gentleman with her had apparently come in. I hung about five minutes; then I went to bed.

I slept badly, for I was agitated. On looking back at these queer occurrences (you will see presently that they were queer), I perhaps suppose myself more agitated than I was; for great anomalies are never so great at first as after we have reflected upon them. It takes us some time to exhaust explanations. I was vaguely nervous – I had been sharply startled; but there was nothing I could not clear up by asking Blanche Adney, the first thing in the morning, who had been with her on the terrace. Oddly enough, however, when the morning dawned – it dawned admirably – I felt less desire to satisfy myself on this point than to escape, to brush away the shadow of my stupefaction. I saw the day would be splendid, and the fancy took me to spend it, as I had spent happy days of youth, in a lonely mountain ramble. I dressed early, partook of conventional coffee, put a big roll into one pocket and a small flask into the other, and, with a stout stick in my hand, went forth into the high places. My story is not closely concerned with the charming hours I passed there – hours of the kind that make intense memories. If I roamed away half of them on the shoulders of the hills, I lay on the sloping grass for the other half and, with my cap pulled over my eyes (save a peep for immensities of view), listened, in the bright stillness, to the mountain bee and felt most things sink and dwindle. Clare Vawdrey grew small, Blanche Adney grew dim, Lord Mellifont grew old, and before the day was over I forgot that I had ever been puzzled. When in the late afternoon I made my way down to the inn there was nothing I wanted so much to find out as whether dinner would not soon be ready. Tonight I dressed, in a manner, and by the time I was presentable they were all at table.

In their company again my little problem came back to me, so that I was curious to see if Vawdrey wouldn't look at me the least bit queerly. But he didn't look at me at all; which gave me a chance both to be patient and to wonder why I should hesitate to ask him my question across the table. I did hesitate, and with the consciousness of doing so came back a little of the agitation I had left behind me, or below me, during the day. I wasn't ashamed of my scruple, however: it was only a fine discretion. What I vaguely felt was that a public inquiry wouldn't have been fair. Lord Mellifont was there, of course, to mitigate with his perfect manner all consequences; but I think it was present to me that with these particular elements his lordship would not be at home. The moment we got up, therefore, I approached Mrs Adney, asking her whether, as the evening was lovely, she wouldn't take a turn with me outside.

'You've walked a hundred miles; had you not better be quiet?' she replied.

'I'd walk a hundred miles more to get you to tell me something.'

She looked at me an instant, with a little of the queerness that I had sought, but had not found, in Clare Vawdrey's eyes. 'Do you mean what became of Lord Mellifont?'

'Of Lord Mellifont?' With my new speculation I had lost that thread.

'Where's your memory, foolish man? We talked of it last evening.'

'Ah, yes!' I cried, recalling; 'we shall have lots to discuss.' I drew her out to the terrace, and before we had gone three steps I said to her: 'Who was with you here last night?'

'Last night?' she repeated, as wide of the mark as I had been.

'At ten o'clock – just after our company broke up. You came out here with a gentleman; you talked about the stars.'

She stared a moment; then she gave her laugh. 'Are you jealous of dear Vawdrey?'

'Then it was he?'

'Certainly it was.'

'And how long did he stay?'

'You have it badly. He stayed about a quarter of an hour – perhaps rather more. We walked some distance; he talked about his play. There you have it all; that is the only witchcraft I have used.'

'And what did Vawdrey do afterwards?'

'I haven't the least idea. I left him and went to bed.'

'At what time did you go to bed?'

'At what time did *you*? I happen to remember that I parted from Mr Vawdrey at ten twenty-five,' said Mrs Adney. 'I came back into the salon to pick up a book, and I noticed the clock.'

'In other words you and Vawdrey distinctly lingered here from about five minutes past ten till the hour you mention?'

'I don't know how distinct we were, but we were very jolly. *Où voulez-vous en venir*[8]?' Blanche Adney asked.

'Simply to this, dear lady: that at the time your companion was occupied in the manner you describe, he was also engaged in literary composition in his own room.'

She stopped short at this, and her eyes had an expression in the darkness. She wanted to know if I challenged her veracity; and I replied that, on the contrary, I backed it up – it made the case so interesting. She returned that this would only be if she should back up mine; which, however, I had no difficulty in persuading her to do, after I had related to her circumstantially the incident of my quest of the manuscript – the manuscript which, at the time, for a reason I could now understand, appeared to have passed so completely out of her own head.

'His talk made me forget it – I forgot I sent you for it. He made up for his fiasco in the salon: he declaimed me the scene,' said my companion. She had dropped on a bench to listen to me and, as we sat there, had briefly cross-examined me. Then she broke out into fresh laughter 'Oh, the eccentricities of genius!'

'They seem greater even than I supposed.'

'Oh, the mysteries of greatness!'

'You ought to know all about them, but they take me by surprise.'

'Are you absolutely certain it was Mr Vawdrey?' my companion asked.

'If it wasn't he, who in the world was it? That a strange gentleman, looking exactly like him, should be sitting in his room at that hour of the night and writing at his table *in the dark*,' I insisted, 'would be practically as wonderful as my own contention.'

'Yes, why in the dark?' mused Mrs Adney.

'Cats can see in the dark,' I said.

She smiled at me dimly. 'Did it look like a cat?'

'No, dear lady, but I'll tell you what it did look like – it looked like the author of Vawdrey's admirable works. It looked infinitely more like him than our friend does himself,' I declared.

'Do you mean it was somebody he gets to do them?'

'Yes, while he dines out and disappoints you.'

'Disappoints me?' murmured Mrs Adney artlessly.

'Disappoints *me* – disappoints everyone who looks in him for the genius that created the pages they adore. Where is it in his talk?'

'Ah, last night he was splendid,' said the actress.

'He's always splendid, as your morning bath is splendid, or a sirloin of beef, or the railway service to Brighton. But he's never rare.'

'I see what you mean.'

'That's what makes you such a comfort to talk to. I've often wondered – now I know. There are two of them.'

'What a delightful idea!'

'One goes out, the other stays at home. One is the genius, the other's the bourgeois, and it's only the bourgeois whom we personally know. He talks, he circulates, he's awfully popular, he flirts with you –'

'Whereas it's the genius *you* are privileged to see!' Mrs Adney broke in. 'I'm much obliged to you for the distinction.'

I laid my hand on her arm. 'See him yourself. Try it, test it, go to his room.'

'Go to his room? It wouldn't be proper!' she exclaimed, in the tone of her best comedy.

'Anything is proper in such an inquiry. If you see him, it settles it.'

'How charming – to settle it!' She thought a moment, then she sprang up. 'Do you mean *now*?'

'Whenever you like.'

'But suppose I should find the wrong one?' said Blanche Adney, with an exquisite effect.

'The wrong one? Which one do you call the right?'

'The wrong one for a lady to go and see. Suppose I shouldn't find – the genius?'

'Oh, I'll look after the other,' I replied. Then, as I had happened to glance about me, I added: 'Take care – here comes Lord Mellifont.'

'I wish you'd look after *him*,' my interlocutress murmured.

'What's the matter with him?'

'That's just what I was going to tell you.'

'Tell me now; he's not coming.'

Blanche Adney looked a moment. Lord Mellifont, who appeared to have emerged from the hotel to smoke a meditative cigar, had paused, at a distance from us, and stood admiring the wonders of the prospect, discernible even in the dusk. We strolled slowly in another direction, and she presently said: 'My idea is almost as droll as yours.'

'I don't call mine droll: it's beautiful.'

'There's nothing so beautiful as the droll,' Mrs Adney declared.

'You take a professional view. But I'm all ears.' My curiosity was indeed alive again.

'Well then, my dear friend, if Clare Vawdrey is double (and I'm bound to say I think that the more of him the better), his lordship there has the opposite complaint: he isn't even whole.'

We stopped once more, simultaneously. 'I don't understand.'

'No more do I. But I have a fancy that if there are two of Mr Vawdrey, there isn't so much as one, all told, of Lord Mellifont.'

I considered a moment, then I laughed out. I think I see what you mean!'

'That's what makes *you* a comfort. Did you ever see him alone?'

I tried to remember. 'Oh, yes; he has been to see me.'

'Ah, then he wasn't alone.'

'And I've been to see him, in his study.'

'Did he know you were there?'

'Naturally – I was announced.'

Blanche Adney glanced at me like a lovely conspirator. 'You mustn't be announced!' With this she walked on.

I rejoined her, breathless. 'Do you mean one must come upon him when he doesn't know it?'

'You must take him unawares. You must go to his room – that's what you must do.'

If I was elated by the way our mystery opened out, I was also, pardonably, a little confused. 'When I know he's not there?'

'When you know he *is*.'

'And what shall I see?'

'You won't see anything!' Mrs Adney cried as we turned round.

We had reached the end of the terrace, and our movement brought us face to face with Lord Mellifont, who, resuming his walk, had now, without indiscretion, overtaken us. The sight of him at that moment was illuminating, and it kindled a great backward train, connecting itself with one's general impression of the personage. As he stood there smiling at us and waving a practised hand into the transparent night (he introduced the view as if it had been a candidate and 'supported' the very Alps), as he rose before us in the delicate fragrance of his cigar and all his other delicacies and fragrances, with more perfections, somehow, heaped upon his handsome head than one had ever seen accumulated before, he struck me as so essentially, so conspicuously and uniformly the public character that I read in a flash the answer to Blanche

Adney's riddle. He was all public and had no corresponding private life, just as Clare Vawdrey was all private and had no corresponding public one. I had heard only half my companion's story, yet as we joined Lord Mellifont (he had followed us – he liked Mrs Adney; but it was always to be conceived of him that he accepted society rather than sought it), as we participated for half an hour in the distributed wealth of his conversation, I felt with unabashed duplicity that we had, as it were, found him out. I was even more deeply diverted by that whisk of the curtain to which the actress had just treated me than I had been by my own discovery; and if I was not ashamed of my share of her secret any more than of having divided my own with her (though my own was, of the two mysteries, the more glorious for the personage involved), this was because there was no cruelty in my advantage, but on the contrary an extreme tenderness and a positive compassion. Oh, he was safe with me, and I felt moreover rich and enlightened, as if I had suddenly put the universe into my pocket. I had learned what an affair of the spot and the moment a great appearance may be. It would doubtless be too much to say that I had always suspected the possibility, in the background of his lordship's being, of some such beautiful instance; but it is at least a fact that, patronizing as it sounds, I had been conscious of a certain reserve of indulgence for him. I had secretly pitied him for the perfection of his performance, had wondered what blank face such a mask had to cover, what was left to him for the immitigable hours in which a man sits down with himself, or, more serious still, with that intenser self, his lawful wife. How was he at home and what did he do when he was alone? There was something in Lady Mellifont that gave a point to these researches – something that suggested that even to her he was still the public character and that she was haunted by similar questionings. She had never cleared them up: that was her eternal trouble. We therefore knew more than she did, Blanche Adney and I; but we wouldn't tell her for the world, nor would she probably thank us for doing so. She preferred the relative grandeur of uncertainty. She was not at home with him, so she couldn't say; and with her he was not alone, so he couldn't show her. He represented to his wife and he was a hero to his servants, and what one wanted to arrive at was what really became of him when no eye could see. He rested, presumably; but what form of rest could repair such a plenitude of presence? Lady Mellifont was too proud to pry, and as she had never looked through a keyhole she remained dignified and unassuaged.

It may have been a fancy of mine that Blanche Adney drew out our companion, or it may be that the practical irony of our relation to him at such a moment made me see him more vividly: at any rate he never had struck me as so dissimilar from what he would have been if we had not offered him a reflection of his image. We were only a concourse of two, but he had never been more public. His perfect manner had never been more perfect, his remarkable tact had never been more remarkable. I had a tacit sense that it would all be in the morning papers, with a leader, and also a secretly exhilarating one that I knew something that wouldn't be, that never could be, though any enterprising journal would give one a fortune for it. I must add, however, that in spite of my enjoyment – it was almost sensual, like that of a consummate dish – I was eager to be alone again with Mrs Adney, who owed me an anecdote. It proved impossible, that evening, for some of the others came out to see what we found so absorbing; and then Lord Mellifont bespoke a little music from the fiddler, who produced his violin and played to us divinely, on our platform of echoes, face to face with the ghosts of the mountains. Before the concert was over I missed our actress and, glancing into the window of the salon, saw that she was established with Vawdrey, who was reading to her from a manuscript. The great scene had apparently been achieved and was doubtless the more interesting to Blanche from the new lights she had gathered about its author. I judged it discreet not to disturb them, and I went to bed without seeing her again. I looked out for her betimes the next morning and, as the promise of the day was fair, proposed to her that we should take to the hills, reminding her of the high obligation she had incurred. She recognised the obligation and gratified me with her company; but before we had strolled ten yards up the pass she broke out with intensity: 'My dear friend, you've no idea how it works in me! I can think of nothing else.'

'Than your theory about Lord Mellifont?'

'Oh, bother Lord Mellifont! I allude to yours about Mr Vawdrey, who is much the more interesting person of the two. I'm fascinated by that vision of his – what-do-you-call-it?'

'His alternative identity?'

'His other self : that's easier to say.'

'You accept it, then, you adopt it?'

'Adopt it? I rejoice in it! It became tremendously vivid to me last evening.'

'While he read to you there?'

'Yes, as I listened to him, watched him. It simplified everything, explained everything.'

'That's indeed the blessing of it. Is the scene very fine?'

'Magnificent, and he reads beautifully.'

'Almost as well as the other one writes!' I laughed.

This made my companion stop a moment, laying her hand on my arm. 'You utter my very impression. I felt that he was reading me the work of another man.'

'What a service to the other man!'

'Such a totally different person,' said Mrs Adney. We talked of this difference as we went on, and of what a wealth it constituted, what a resource for life, such a duplication of character.

'It ought to make him live twice as long as other people,' I observed.

'Ought to make which of them?'

'Well, both; for after all they're members of a firm, and one of them couldn't carry on the business without the other. Moreover mere survival would be dreadful for either.'

Blanche Adney was silent a little; then she exclaimed: 'I don't know – I wish he *would* survive!'

'May I, on my side, enquire which?'

'If you can't guess I won't tell you.'

'I know the heart of woman. You always prefer the other.'

She halted again, looking round her. 'Off here, away from my husband, I *can* tell you. I'm in love with him!'

'Unhappy woman, he has no passions,' I answered.

'That's exactly why I adore him. Doesn't a woman with my history know that the passions of others are insupportable? An actress, poor thing, can't care for any love that's not all on *her* side; she can't afford to be repaid. My marriage proves that: marriage is ruinous. Do you know what was in my mind last night, all the while Mr Vawdrey was reading me those beautiful speeches? An insane desire to see the author.' And dramatically, as if to hide her shame, Blanche Adney passed on.

'We'll manage that,' I returned. 'I want another glimpse of him myself. But meanwhile please remember that I've been waiting more than forty-eight hours for the evidence that supports your sketch, intensely suggestive and plausible, of Lord Mellifont's private life.'

'Oh, Lord Mellifont doesn't interest me.'

'He did yesterday,' I said.

'Yes, but that was before I fell in love. You blotted him out with your story.'

'You'll make me sorry I told it. Come,' I pleaded, 'if you don't let me know how your idea came into your head I shall imagine you simply made it up.'

'Let me recollect then, while we wander in this grassy valley.'

We stood at the entrance of a charming crooked gorge, a portion of whose level floor formed the bed of a stream that was smooth with swiftness. We turned into it, and the soft walk beside the clear torrent drew us on and on; till suddenly, as we continued and I waited for my companion to remember, a bend of the valley showed us Lady Mellifont coming toward us. She was alone, under the canopy of her parasol, drawing her sable train over the turf; and in this form, on the devious ways, she was a sufficiently rare apparition. She usually took a footman, who marched behind her on the highroads and whose livery was strange to the mountaineers. She blushed on seeing us, as if she ought somehow to justify herself; she laughed vaguely and said she had come out for a little early stroll. We stood together a moment, exchanging platitudes, and then she remarked that she had thought she might find her husband.

'Is he in this quarter?' I enquired.

'I supposed he would be. He came out an hour ago to sketch.'

'Have you been looking for him?' Mrs Adney asked.

'A little; not very much,' said Lady Mellifont.

Each of the women rested her eyes with some intensity, as it seemed to me, on the eyes of the other.

'We'll look for him *for* you, if you like,' said Mrs Adney.

'Oh, it doesn't matter. I thought I'd join him.'

'He won't make his sketch if you don't,' my companion hinted.

'Perhaps he will if *you* do,' said Lady Mellifont.

'Oh, I dare say he'll turn up,' I interposed.

'He certainly will if he knows we're here!' Blanche Adney retorted.

'Will you wait while we search?' I asked of Lady Mellifont.

She repeated that it was of no consequence; upon which Mrs Adney went on: 'We'll go into the matter for our own pleasure.'

'I wish you a pleasant expedition,' said her ladyship, and was turning away when I sought to know if we should inform her husband that she had followed him. She hesitated a moment; then she jerked out oddly: 'I think you had better not.' With this she took leave of us, floating a little stiffly down the gorge.

My companion and I watched her retreat, then we exchanged a stare, while a light ghost of a laugh rippled from the actress's lips. 'She might be walking in the shrubberies at Mellifont!'

'She suspects it, you know,' I replied.

'And she doesn't want him to know it. There won't be any sketch.'

'Unless we overtake him,' I subjoined. 'In that case we shall find him producing one, in the most graceful attitude, and the queer thing is that it will be brilliant.'

'Let us leave him alone – he'll have to come home without it.'

'He'd rather never come home. Oh, he'll find a public!'

'Perhaps he'll do it for the cows,' Blanche Adney suggested; and as I was on the point of rebuking her profanity she went on: 'That's simply what I happened to discover.'

'What are you speaking of?'

'The incident of day before yesterday.'

'Ah, let's have it at last!'

'That's all it was – that I was like Lady Mellifont: I couldn't find him.'

'Did you lose him?'

'He lost *me* – that appears to be the way of it. He thought I was gone.'

'But you did find him, since you came home with him.'

'It was he who found *me*. That again is what must happen. He's there from the moment he knows somebody else is.'

'I understand his intermissions,' I said after a short reflection, 'but I don't quite seize the law that governs them.'

'Oh, it's a fine shade, but I caught it at that moment. I had started to come home. I was tired, and I had insisted on his not coming back with me. We had found some rare flowers – those I brought home – and it was he who had discovered almost all of them. It amused him very much, and I knew he wanted to get more; but I was weary and I quitted him. He let me go – where else would have been his tact? – and I was too stupid then to have guessed that from the moment I was not there no flower would be gathered. I started homeward, but at the end of three minutes I found I had brought away his penknife – he had lent it to me to trim a branch – and I knew he would need it. I turned back a few steps, to call him, but before I spoke I looked about for him. You can't understand what happened then without having the place before you.'

'You must take me there,' I said.

'We may see the wonder here. The place was simply one that offered no chance for concealment – a great gradual hillside, without obstructions or trees. There were some rocks below me, behind which I myself had disappeared, but from which on coming back I immediately emerged again.'

'Then he must have seen you.'

'He was too utterly gone, for some reason best known to himself. It was probably some moment of fatigue – he's getting on, you know, so that, with the sense of returning solitude, the reaction had been proportionately great, the extinction proportionately complete. At any rate the stage was as bare as your hand.'

'Could he have been somewhere else?'

'He couldn't have been, in the time, anywhere but where I had left him. Yet the place was utterly empty – as empty as this stretch of valley before us. He had vanished – he had ceased to be. But as soon as my voice rang out (I uttered his name), he rose before me like the rising sun.'

'And where did the sun rise?'

'Just where it ought to – just where he would have been and where I should have seen him had he been like other people.'

I had listened with the deepest interest, but it was my duty to think of objections. 'How long a time elapsed between the moment you perceived his absence and the moment you called?'

'Oh, only an instant. I don't pretend it was long.'

'Long enough for you to be sure?' I said.

'Sure he wasn't there?'

'Yes, and that you were not mistaken, not the victim of some hocus-pocus of your eyesight.'

'I may have been mistaken, but I don't believe it. At any rate, that's just why I want you to look in his room.'

I thought a moment. 'How *can* I, when even his wife doesn't dare to?'

'She *wants* to; propose it to her. It wouldn't take much to make her. She does suspect.'

I thought another moment. 'Did he seem to know?'

'That I had missed him? So it struck me, but he thought he had been quick enough.'

'Did you speak of his disappearance?'

'Heaven forbid! It seemed to me too strange.'

'Quite right. And how did he look?'

Trying to think it out again and reconstitute her miracle, Blanche Adney gazed abstractedly up the valley. Suddenly she exclaimed: 'Just as he looks now!' and I saw Lord Mellifont stand before us with his sketch-block. I perceived, as we met him, that he looked neither suspicious nor blank: he looked simply, as he did always, everywhere, the principal feature of the scene. Naturally he had no sketch to show us, but nothing could better have rounded off our actual conception of him than the way he fell into position as we approached. He had been selecting his point of view; he took possession of it with a flourish of the pencil. He leaned against a rock; his beautiful little box of water-colours reposed on a natural table beside him, a ledge of the bank which showed how inveterately nature ministered to his convenience. He painted while he talked and he talked while he painted; and if the painting was as miscellaneous as the talk, the talk would equally have graced an album. We waited while the exhibition went on, and it seemed indeed as if the conscious profiles of the peaks were interested in his success. They grew as black as silhouettes in paper, sharp against a livid sky from which, however, there would be nothing to fear till Lord Mellifont's sketch should be finished. Blanche Adney communed with me dumbly, and I could read the language of her eyes: 'Oh, if *we* could only do it as well as that! He fills the stage in a way that beats us.' We could no more have left him than we could have quitted the theatre till the play was over; but in due time we turned round with him and strolled back to the inn, before the door of which his lordship, glancing again at his picture, tore the fresh leaf from the block and presented it with a few happy words to Mrs Adney. Then he went into the house; and a moment later, looking up from where we stood, we saw him, above, at the window of his sitting-room (he had the best apartments), watching the signs of the weather.

'He'll have to rest after this,' Blanche said, dropping her eyes on her water-colour.

'Indeed he will!' I raised mine to the window: Lord Mellifont had vanished. 'He's already reabsorbed.'

'Reabsorbed?' I could see the actress was now thinking of something else.

'Into the immensity of things. He has lapsed again; there's an entr'acte[9].'

'It ought to be long.' Mrs Adney looked up and down the terrace, and at that moment the head-waiter appeared in the doorway. Suddenly she turned to this functionary with the question: 'Have you seen Mr Vawdrey lately?'

The man immediately approached. 'He left the house five minutes ago – for a walk, I think. He went down the pass; he had a book.'

I was watching the ominous clouds. 'He had better have had an umbrella.'

The waiter smiled. 'I recommended him to take one.'

'Thank you,' said Mrs Adney; and the Oberkellner[10] withdrew. Then she went on, abruptly: 'Will you do me a favour?'

'Yes, if you'll do *me* one. Let me see if your picture is signed.'

She glanced at the sketch before giving it to me. 'For a wonder it isn't.'

'It ought to be, for full value. May I keep it awhile?'

'Yes, if you'll do what I ask. Take an umbrella and go after Mr Vawdrey.'

'To bring him to Mrs Adney?'

'To keep him out – as long as you can.'

'I'll keep him as long as the rain holds off.'

'Oh, never mind the rain!' my companion exclaimed.

'Would you have us drenched?'

'Without remorse.' Then with a strange light in her eyes she added: 'I'm going to try.'

'To try?'

'To see the real one. Oh, if I can get at him!' she broke out with passion.

'Try, try!' I replied. 'I'll keep our friend all day.'

'If I can get at the one who does it' – and she paused, with shining eyes – 'if I can have it out with him I shall get my part!'

'I'll keep Vawdrey for ever!' I called after her as she passed quickly into the house.

Her audacity was communicative, and I stood there in a glow of excitement. I looked at Lord Mellifont's watercolour and I looked at the gathering storm; I turned my eyes again to his lordship's windows and then I bent them on my watch. Vawdrey had so little the start of me that I should have time to overtake him – time even if I should take five minutes to go up to Lord Mellifont's sitting-room (where we had all been hospitably received), and say to him, as a messenger, that Mrs Adney begged he would bestow upon his sketch the high consecration of his signature. As I again considered this work of art I perceived there was something it certainly did lack: what else then but so noble an autograph? It was my duty to supply the deficiency without delay, and in accordance with this conviction I instantly re-entered the hotel. I went up to Lord Mellifont's apartments; I reached the door of his salon.

Here, however, I was met by a difficulty of which my extravagance had not taken account. If I were to knock I should spoil everything; yet was I prepared to dispense with this ceremony? I asked myself the question, and it embarrassed me; I turned my little picture round and round, but it didn't give me the answer I wanted. I wanted it to say: 'Open the door gently, gently, without a sound, yet very quickly: then you will see what you will see.' I had gone so far as to lay my hand upon the knob when I became aware (having my wits so about me), that exactly in the manner I was thinking of – gently, gently, without a sound – another door had moved, on the opposite side of the hall. At the same instant I found myself smiling rather constrainedly upon Lady Mellifont, who, on seeing me, had checked herself on the threshold of her room. For a moment, as she stood there, we exchanged two or three ideas that were the more singular for being unspoken. We had caught each other hovering, and we understood each other; but as I stepped over to her (so that we were separated from the sitting-room by the width of the hall), her lips formed the almost soundless entreaty: 'Don't!'[I could see in her conscious eyes everything that the word expressed – the confession of her own curiosity and the dread of the consequences of mine. '*Don't!*' she repeated, as I stood before her. From the moment my experiment could strike her as an act of violence I was ready to renounce it; yet I thought I detected in her frightened face a still deeper betrayal – a possibility of disappointment if I should give way. It was as if she had said: 'I'll let you do it if you'll take the responsibility. Yes, with someone else I'd surprise him. But it would never do for him to think it was I.'

'We soon found Lord Mellifont,' I observed, in allusion to our encounter with her an hour before, 'and he was so good as to give this lovely sketch to Mrs Adney, who has asked me to come up and beg him to put in the omitted signature.'

Lady Mellifont took the drawing from me, and I could guess the struggle that went on in her while she looked at it. She was silent for some time; then I felt that all her delicacies and dignities, all her old timidities and pieties were fighting against her opportunity. She turned away from me and, with the drawing, went back to her room. She was absent for a couple of minutes, and when she reappeared I could see that she had vanquished her temptation; that even, with a kind of resurgent horror, she had shrunk from it. She had deposited the sketch in the room. 'If you will kindly leave the picture with me, I will see that Mrs Adney's request is attended to,' she said, with great courtesy and sweetness, but in a manner that put an end to our colloquy.

I assented, with a somewhat artificial enthusiasm perhaps, and then, to ease off our separation, remarked that we were going to have a change of weather.

'In that case we shall go – we shall go immediately,' said Lady Mellifont. I was amused at the eagerness with which she made this declaration: it appeared to represent a coveted flight into safety, an escape with her threatened secret. I was the more surprised therefore when, as I was turning away, she put out her hand to take mine. She had the pretext of bidding me farewell, but as I shook hands with her on this supposition I felt that what the movement really conveyed was: 'I thank you for the help you would have given me, but it's better as it is. If I should know, who would help me then?' As I went to my room to get my umbrella I said to myself : 'She's sure, but she won't put it to the proof.'

A quarter of an hour later I had overtaken Clare Vawdrey in the pass, and shortly after this we found ourselves looking for refuge. The storm had not only completely gathered, but it had broken at the last with extraordinary rapidity. We scrambled up a hillside to an empty cabin, a rough structure that was hardly more than a shed for the protection of cattle. It was a tolerable shelter however, and it had fissures through which we could watch the splendid spectacle of the tempest. This entertainment lasted an hour – an hour that has remained with me as full of odd disparities. While the lightning played with the thunder and the rain gushed in on our umbrellas, I said to myself that Clare Vawdrey was disappointing. I don't know exactly what I should have predicated of a great author exposed to the fury of the elements, I can't say what particular Manfred attitude I should have expected my companion to assume, but it seemed to me somehow that I shouldn't have looked to him to regale me in such a situation with stories (which I had already heard), about the celebrated Lady Ringrose. Her ladyship formed the subject of Vawdrey's conversation during this prodigious scene, though before it was quite over he had launched out on Mr Chafer, the scarcely less notorious reviewer. It broke my heart to hear a man like Vawdrey talk of reviewers. The lightning projected a hard clearness upon the truth, familiar to me for years, to which the last day or two had added transcendent support – the irritating certitude that for personal relations this admirable genius thought his second-best good enough. It *was*, no doubt, as society was made, but there was a contempt in the distinction which could not fail to be galling to an admirer. The world was vulgar and stupid, and the real man would have been a fool to come out for it when he could gossip and dine by deputy. Nonetheless my heart sank as I felt my companion practise this economy. I don't know exactly what I wanted; I suppose I wanted him to make an exception for *me*. I almost believed he would, if he had known how I worshipped his talent. But I had never been able to translate this to him, and his application of his principle was relentless. At any rate I was more than ever sure that at such an hour his chair at home was not empty: *there* was the Manfred attitude, *there* were the responsive flashes. I could only envy Mrs Adney her presumable enjoyment of them.

The weather drew off at last, and the rain abated sufficiently to allow us to emerge from our asylum and make our way back to the inn, where we found on our arrival that our prolonged absence had produced some agitation. It was judged apparently that the fury of the elements might have placed us in a predicament. Several of our friends were at the door, and they seemed a little disconcerted when it was perceived that we were only drenched. Clare Vawdrey, for some reason, was wetter than I, and he took his course to his room. Blanche Adney was among the persons collected to look out for us, but as Vawdrey came toward her she shrank from him, without a greeting; with a movement that I observed as almost one of estrangement she turned her back on him and went quickly into the salon. Wet as I was I went in after her; on which she immediately flung round and faced me. The first thing I saw was that she had never been so beautiful. There was a light of inspiration in her face, and she broke out to me in the quickest whisper, which was at the same time the loudest cry, I have ever heard: 'I've got my *part!*'

'You went to his room – I was right?'

'Right?' Blanche Adney repeated. 'Ah, my dear fellow!' she murmured.

'He was there – you saw him?'

'He saw me. It was the hour of my life!'

'It must have been the hour of his, if you were half as lovely as you are at this moment.'

'He's splendid,' she pursued, as if she didn't hear me. 'He is the one who does it!' I listened, immensely impressed, and she added: 'We understood each other.'

'By flashes of lightning?'

'Oh, I didn't see the lightning then!'

'How long were you there?' I asked with admiration.

'Long enough to tell him I adore him.'

'Ah, that's what I've never been able to tell him!' I exclaimed ruefully.

'I shall have my part – I shall have my part!' she continued, with triumphant indifference; and she flung round the room with the joy of a girl, only checking herself to say: 'Go and change your clothes.'

'You shall have Lord Mellifont's signature,' I said.

'Oh, bother Lord Mellifont's signature! He's far nicer than Mr Vawdrey,' she went on irrelevantly.

'Lord Mellifont?' I pretended to enquire.

'Confound Lord Mellifont!' And Blanche Adney, in her elation, brushed by me, whisking again through the open door. Just outside of it she came upon her husband; whereupon, with a charming cry of 'We're talking of you, my love!' she threw herself upon him and kissed him.

I went to my room and changed my clothes, but I remained there till the evening. The violence of the storm had passed over us, but the rain had settled down to a drizzle. On descending to dinner I found that the change in the weather had already broken up our party. The Mellifonts had departed in a carriage and four, they had been followed by others, and several vehicles had been bespoken for the morning. Blanche Adney's was one of them, and on the pretext that she had preparations to make she quitted us directly after dinner. Clare Vawdrey asked me what was the matter with her – she suddenly appeared to dislike him. I forget what answer I gave, but I did my best to comfort him by driving away with him the next day. Mrs Adney had vanished when we came down; but they made up their quarrel in London, for he finished his play, which she produced. I must add that she is still, nevertheless, in want of the great part. I have a beautiful one in my head, but she doesn't come to see me to stir me up about it. Lady Mellifont always drops me a kind word when we meet, but that doesn't console me.

NOTES

1. Originally in classical Roman mythology, a house's protective deity. Has come to mean more literally 'the spirit of a place'.
2. Included (French).
3. Early children's primer, usually featuring letters of the alphabet, so-named due to the sheet of horn that covered and protected the text.
4. French expression, loosely equivalent to 'pick of the crop' or 'finest flower'.
5. Dining room (French).
6. 'Dear Master' (French).
7. Green beans (French).
8. 'What are you driving at?' (French).
9. Interval (French).
10. Head waiter (German).

BIOGRAPHICAL NOTE

Henry James, novelist, playwright, short-story writer and critic, was born in New York in 1843. Educated in France, Germany and Switzerland, he attended Harvard Law School in 1862, later travelling extensively across Europe – an experience that prompted his first published books, two volumes of travel essays in 1875. His first published novel, *Roderick Hudson*, appeared the following year, depicting an American's moral decline when in Rome, and relations between America and Europe formed the themes of further works, anticipating *The Portrait of a Lady* (1881).

From 1887, James lived in London, remaining there – his many European trips notwithstanding – until 1896, when he moved to Rye. His focus shifted to an exclusively English arena with his 1890 novel, *The Tragic Muse*, in which he explored the notion of the English character. He went on to pen biographies, literary criticism and the fragment of autobiography, *A Small Boy and Others* (1913), but in his later novels – *The Wings of the Dove* (1902), *The Ambassadors* (1903) and *The Golden Bowl* (1904) – he again returned to differences between America and Europe.

Today renowned as a master stylist whose novels often elaborate a moral consciousness torn between individual and social obligations, Henry James wrote with care and precision about Western civilisation as he understood it. Writing at a period when the novel form was reaching the heights of its sophistication, James critically examined the genre in his *The Art of Fiction* (1885), and praised Balzac above all other nineteenth-century novelists as 'the master of us all'. He assumed British nationality in 1915, dying the following year after suffering a stroke.